WEST SIDE GORY

book six of the matchmaker mysteries series

elise sax

ISBN: 978-1548050566
Published in the United States by 13 Lakes Publishing

Cover design: Sprinkles On Top Studios
Edited by: Novel Needs
Formatted by: Jesse Kimmel-Freeman

Printed in the United States of America

elisesax.com
elisesax@gmail.com
http://elisesax.com/mailing-list.php
https://www.facebook.com/ei.sax.9

For Max because he wants to live his passion, and I know he will.

ALSO BY ELISE SAX

CHAPTER 1

Matches come to us because they feel that something's missing. They've been looking, but they can't find it on their own, so they ask us to do it for them. Find the missing. That's what we do. Is it here? Is it there? Who knows? We do, bubeleh. At least, we're supposed to. But here's the thing, dolly: Sometimes a match thinks that love is missing when it's been right there with them the whole time. Also, sometimes a match thinks that love is there with them when it's been missing the whole time. So, focus on the missing. Study what's not there. Start with the hole and work your way out.

Lesson 6, Matchmaking advice from your Grandma Zelda

"I'm having sex," I said, smiling. I had been smiling for days. "A lot of it."

"I know, dolly. I got a white noise machine so I can sleep because of all your sex activities. Pass the cream cheese."

I passed my grandmother the tub of cream cheese. I poured myself a second cup of coffee and directed my smile at Spencer. He was sitting at the kitchen table with Grandma and me, eating an everything bagel with grape jelly. He took huge bites, washing it down with cream-laden coffee.

"She's looking at me again, Zelda," he told my grandmother with his mouth full.

"You're a lot to see," she said.

She was right. Spencer was a lot to see. He was wearing black sweatpants that hugged low on his hips, nothing on his feet, and no shirt. Spencer's muscles bulged as he lifted the bagel to his mouth. His shoulders were wide and enormous, and he had no belly where his belly should have been, only a washboard of muscles. When he moved the cup of coffee, his back undulated, his large muscles dancing. I reached out and touched his back, and a giggle erupted from my mouth.

"I'm having sex," I told my grandmother again.

"I'm going to make eggs. Anybody want eggs?" Spencer stood, leaned over, and gave me a kiss. With tongue. I sighed into his mouth.

"Two over easy," Grandma told him.

We had settled into a routine since Spencer and I had settled into each other. He had more or less moved into my bedroom, and Grandma had welcomed us as a couple into her house, into her life. We had breakfast together every morning at seven and dinner at six. We were like the Waltons, except that I was pretty sure that Mrs. Walton had never had sex in the shower.

But I had.

Twice that morning.

Spencer threw some butter in a pan and cracked the eggs.

"Bubeleh, you're going to have to tamper down your smile today," my grandmother told me. "With Valentine's Day around the corner, the matchless matches are surging."

"Surging?"

She nodded, sadly. "Like the first wave at Gallipoli. There'll be a lot of casualties. That's why I'm going to try and head them off with my chocolate-making and flower arranging classes."

Spencer put two eggs on Grandma's plate and three on his. He slipped the pan into the sink and took his seat, again. "Smart plan, Zelda," he said, waving his fork at her. "Surround them with chocolate and flowers so they don't realize that they weren't given any chocolate and flowers."

I smiled and touched his back again, tracing the lines of his muscles. It was my first Valentine's Day with Spencer, my first Valentine's Day in years where I was in a relationship, and I would have bet money that I was going to get chocolate and flowers. Spencer shot me a look and winked at me. I could feel my face turn red, and it was all I could do not to drag him back into the shower.

Spencer sopped up the rest of his eggs with a piece of bagel and popped it into his mouth. "We're here, Zelda!" A woman sing-songed, as the front door opened, and the click-clack of sensible heels marched toward us in the kitchen. "I've got the chocolate molds," the woman announced. She was holding two large, plastic bags filled with chocolate molds, but she dropped them when she got a look at Spencer's naked torso.

The molds crashed to the linoleum floor, and the woman stumbled backward, knocking into the wall. Three more women piled into the kitchen and also suffered various reactions to seeing half-naked Spencer. It wasn't the first time that this had happened. He tried to get dressed by eight every morning, but sometimes people showed up early, and even when he was fully dressed, Spencer had a certain effect on women. It was sort of like a strobe light, provoking seizures.

Since my grandmother's house was in the heart of our town of Cannes, California, where people came and went to be matched and to handle the town's business, there was a steady stream of women having reactions to Spencer's hotness.

"We're not dressed yet," I told the women, who were staring at Spencer in a catatonic state. For his part, he ignored them and downed the rest of his coffee and wiped his mouth with a napkin. After a few weeks, he had become accustomed to the women's reactions, and he took them in stride. He stood and went to the sink to wash his dishes. His sweatpants hung low on his hips, baring all kinds of wonderful. Spencer was a metrosexual, always perfectly dressed, but wearing next to nothing with his hair messed had to be his best look.

"We're not dressed, yet," Grandma agreed. She was wearing a housedress and slippers. I was the only one who was ready for the day in jeans and a gray cashmere sweater that I had stolen from Spencer. I had an appointment in a few minutes with my friends Lucy and Bridget to do wedding stuff. Lucy was getting married on Valentine's Day, and her wedding was going to be crazy over-the-top. Even though she had hired a large army to help with the event, she still needed my help with wedding errands.

Spencer put his dishes in the drainer and turned around. "Good morning, ladies," he said to the chocolate women, giving them his most dashing smile and a slight bow. Walking around the table, he grabbed my hand, yanking me up from my chair. "If you'll excuse us."

He wrapped his arms around my waist and pushed me out the door, his body up against my back. As soon as we got halfway up the stairs, he pulled me in close and gave me a kiss, which would have impregnated me, if I hadn't been on the Pill.

"Don't get into trouble today," he said, his big blue eyes studying my face for any trouble-making plans.

"I'm just going out with Lucy and Bridget to do wedding stuff."

He arched an eyebrow. "Don't get into trouble."

"I think we're looking at her rehearsal dinner cake. I never knew weddings could have so many dinners and cakes."

"No trouble." His eyes were dark, bottomless pools. They made my hormones jump around in my how-do-you-do, like Mexican jumping beans.

"I don't think anyone's ever gotten into trouble looking at a cake."

"Please, no trouble."

"You're not the boss of me," I said. His lips dared to differ. They found my neck and trailed kisses down to my collar bone. I moaned Spencer's name, and he stopped kissing me, putting his hands on my shoulders to steady me so I wouldn't fall down the stairs in an aroused heap. "Okay, so you're kind of the boss of me," I breathed.

Then, my feminist sensibilities took over. I stomped my foot on the stair. "You're not the boss of me."

Spencer smirked. "So, you won't dress up as my secretary tonight? A nurse to my doctor?"

That sounded good. "No," I lied.

Spencer's smirk grew, and a dimple appeared on his cheek. "Nurse, come here. Stat. Take off your clothes. Stat. Come on, Pinky. Don't you want to "stat" with me? We could stat all night long. I could make your toes curl."

I liked it when he made my toes curl. He made my toes curl a lot. In fact, they started to curl right there on the stairs.

"I might let you make my toes curl," I said.

"It's a date." His blue eyes lasered in on my eyes. His face had a perfect level of stubble, and his pecs flexed. He kissed me again. This time it was soft and gentle, his tongue loving mine in long sweeps. When it ended, he smirked again and gently slapped my butt. "No trouble," he repeated and ran up the stairs, taking them two at a time.

"Oh," I moaned and rubbed a hand down my face to make sure I was still there and hadn't evaporated into a cloud of hormones.

"Holy smokes," someone said below me. I looked down to find the entranceway filled with Grandma's matches and my friend Lucy, and they were all looking up at me.

One of the matches pulled her checkbook and a pen out of her purse and waved it at me. "I'll give you six-hundred-fifteen-dollars and thirty-two cents if you let me kiss him next time," she said. "More if you give me an advance on my next pay day."

I should have taken her up on her offer. I had thirty-five dollars in the bank, and my new car was running on fumes. But curled toes took the sting out of being poor, so I declined the offer.

"I'm sorry. We're going steady," I said.

It was the wrong thing to say to a group of women who were going to make homemade chocolate to distract themselves from the fact that they were alone for Valentine's. I felt the room turn on me. There was a definite wave of animosity aimed in my direction. Grandma had been right about laying low during the Valentine's season. It was outright dangerous to flaunt the fact that I was involved with the best-looking man in Cannes. I had put my life on the line.

"You know, all that sex can make your vagina fall out," one of the women announced, none too charitably.

"What?" I asked.

"That's true," another woman said. "I knew a woman like that. She was taking a shower and *plop!* her vagina fell out, just like she dropped the soap or something."

My knees knocked against each other, and I squeezed my thighs tight. Yikes, I didn't want my vagina to fall out. Was that the punishment for falling in love?

Lucy happily slapped the back of the woman who compared my vagina to a bar of soap. "Isn't it a glorious day, darlin'? The lilies are in bloom."

Since it was the middle of February, I doubted there were any lilies in bloom, but Lucy definitely was. After years of being single and a powerhouse in marketing—whatever that was—she was about to marry Uncle Harry, who wasn't actually her uncle or anyone related to her. He was a man of uncertain age and profession with no obvious signs of a neck. She had been floating on cloud nine since he proposed, and she had been planning a wedding that cost about the same as Guatemala's GDP. I was her maid of honor.

Lucy was wearing a neck-to-ankle fur coat and fur hat. Her pretty face was flushed from the cold outside and the thrill of her impending super-party. I walked down the stairs. "Can my vagina really fall out?" I whispered to her.

"Don't worry. I bet it can take a real pounding,

darlin'," she whispered back.

It wasn't quite the "no way" that I was looking for. Spencer came downstairs. He was now wearing one of his tailored suits, and he looked like he was ready to walk the red carpet at the Emmys.

"I gotta run," he said, opening the coat closet. "You won't believe this one, but this crazy town has a problem with a pack of wild Chihuahuas." He threw his coat on, kissed me, and ran out the front door.

"I heard about that pack of Chihuahuas," one of the women told me when Spencer left. "They cornered a friend of mine outside of Burger Boy. She had to toss them her double cheeseburger with extra bacon to get away."

Another woman nodded. "I don't go anywhere now without a raw steak in my purse. You know, just to be safe." She pulled the steak out of her purse to show us.

"You couldn't blow me out of this loony town with a hydrogen bomb," Lucy whispered in my ear. "I would be so bored anywhere else."

Grandma walked in and ordered her matches to set up the chocolate-making class in the kitchen. With Spencer gone, they were finally able to focus on not focusing about their lack of dates for Valentine's.

"Are you ready to do wedding things?" Lucy asked me

when we were alone.

"Yes, I just have to get my shoes."

"Is Bridget here?"

"No, she's called me to tell me that she's running late," I said.

Lucy smiled a magnanimous smile, like she was Cleopatra and the progress on her latest pyramid was going well. "No problem. We'll wait. No hurry."

Despite her laid back attitude, Lucy's wedding was a notch above Princess Diana's in pomp and circumstance and it had to be stressful to plan. Even Eisenhower had to have had an out-of-control moment or two when he was planning D-Day. So far, Lucy hadn't gone off the deep end, but I didn't want to tempt any bridezilla moments with her. So, whatever she wanted me to do, I did, pronto. I ran upstairs to get my shoes and put them on as quickly as I could so she wouldn't wait long. Running back downstairs, I found my shearling coat in the closet and put it on.

"There. Done," I said, brightly. "All ready to do wedding things."

Actually, I had no idea how to do wedding things. Wedding things and I didn't mix. Sure, I had worked as a professional witness at Al's Takeout Nuptials in Reno for a month, but I wouldn't categorize Al's—where a couple could get married and get a bucket of chicken to go for $49.99—as wedding things.

The front door burst open, and my other best friend Bridget entered. She was frazzled. Her hoot owl glasses had fallen halfway down her nose, and her coat was hanging off one shoulder. She had added extra blue eye shadow this morning, and it was bleeding around her eyes. Her hair hit her shoulders in long ringlets. She was about five months pregnant, and she was just starting to get a little baby bump. She looked around and skidded to a stop just before she ran into Lucy and me.

"Am I late? Am I late? I'm so sorry," she said, huffing and puffing.

"Right on time," Lucy said.

"What's the matter?" I asked. "Were you out protesting?" Bridget was anti-just about everything, and she was happiest when she was protesting.

"No. Not even. I was working." Bridget was a bookkeeper and handled the books for pretty much everyone in town. "Tax season has started, and people are nervous, Gladie. Real nervous. Barry at Hardware Barry's wanted to deduct his suits. Well, I can't let that happen, and even if I wanted to, little Vladimir gives me a good kick every time I play fast and loose with the federal tax code."

"Your baby knows the tax code?" I asked.

Bridget nodded. "It must be the Baby Einstein videos I've been watching."

Lucy put her perfectly manicured hand on Bridget's arm. "Darlin', you can't name that child, Vladimir."

"For Vladimir Lenin…"

Bridget had been going through a list of labor activists' names for her unborn child.

"He will get his butt kicked every day for years. Do you want that on your head? What happened to Cesar Chavez? You liked that name," Lucy reminded her.

Bridget gnawed on her lip. "Yes, but I'm worried that that would be cultural appropriation, and I don't speak Spanish."

"You're Irish," I reminded her. "Wasn't Lenin Russian?" Okay, I was the first to admit that I was uneducated, but even I knew who Lenin was. And the name Vladimir sounded like he was building monsters in Transylvania or something. Still, I knew better than to criticize a parent. If brides were ornery, mothers-to-be were downright dangerous. So, as far as I was concerned, Bridget could name her son anything she wanted.

"Names are hard," Bridget said. "If it was a girl, it

would be easier. She would be Gloria Hillary Abzug Sanger Donovan. Doesn't that sound wonderful?"

"Practically trips over the tongue," Lucy said. "Come on. Bring Vladimir, and let's get going."

Outside, we piled into Lucy's Mercedes, which was parked in the driveway next to my new, used Oldsmobile Cutlass Supreme. My grandmother's house was in the heart of Cannes's Historic District. Cannes was a small town in the mountains east of San Diego and had been settled in the 1800s when gold was discovered. But the gold quickly ran out, leaving behind the Historic District, which was now mostly antique stores and pie shops, which brought in the tourists. The town was surrounded by apple and pear orchards and about half of the country's retirees.

"I'm having sex," I announced, as we turned onto Main Street.

"With a hot cop. So you keep telling us. It's your number one conversation topic. That and the chicken sandwich at Burger Boy." Lucy said. The new chicken sandwich had double-fried chicken, bacon, three kinds of cheese, with a doughnut bun. Who wouldn't want to talk about that?

"I'd like to have sex," Bridget said, rubbing her belly. "I've got big time hormones, like nuclear waste estrogen or Spiderman estrogen. Yesterday, I got turned on in the market in the cereal aisle. It's pretty desperate when you get aroused by spoon-sized shredded wheat."

I remembered that my grandmother warned me about talking about my sex life to those who weren't hitting the sheets. I would have to get Bridget some chocolate as soon as I could to try and tamper down her Spiderman estrogen.

"Do you want to stop at Tea Time for a latte?" Lucy asked me. Tea Time was a tea shop housed in an old saloon, and it was run by Ruth, an ornery octogenarian who hated coffee drinkers. Despite that, she made the best coffee in the world, and I had made a deal with her for free lattes for a year.

"Maybe after the bakery," I said.

"Wow, you're the calmest bride I've ever seen," Bridget said. "Your wedding is next week, but you're cool as a cucumber. You don't even mind taking time out of your wedding errands to get Gladie a latte. I'm impressed."

Lucy waved dismissively, her smile never wavering. "Why should I be anxious? I'm marrying the man of my dreams. Even if everything goes wrong with the wedding, I'm still marrying him. And what can go wrong? This wedding is planned to the T. I've put Martha Stewart to shame, I'm so organized. Not to mention, I'm now unemployed, and I love being unemployed."

"No more marketing?" Bridget asked.

"No more marketing," Lucy sang. "No more travel. No more catering to old, smelly men." Her fiancé was old and smelly, but just like not talking about my sex life, I decided to keep quiet about that. "We're building our dream home, and it should be done when we get back from our cruise."

As far as I was concerned, Lucy already lived in a dream house and so did Uncle Harry. They had more money than they knew what to do with, and they each owned a mansion. But I was happy that Lucy had found an ideal life with him, and they deserved to plan whatever they wanted with each other.

"Here we are," Lucy said, parking on the street in front of the bakery.

An intricate sign in white announced that it was the Happily Ever After Bakery. The storefront was also in white wood paneling, carved like it was a large cake. Lucy locked her car, and we walked inside.

We were the only customers in the shop, which smelled like sugar, flour, and heaven. It was wedding all over the place with shelves of plastic figures to put on top of cakes. Inside a large glass case, which spanned the width of the shop, were mini-wedding cakes.

"Those are taster cakes," Lucy explained. "Uncle Harry and I must have tasted twenty before we decided on the rum raisin with the chocolate peppermint ganache."

Rum raisin with chocolate peppermint ganache sounded disgusting to me, but more than anything, I wanted to get into the case and taste twenty cakes. "Are we going to lunch today? I could go for lunch," I said, staring at the cakes.

"You just ate," Lucy said and then waved her hands, like she was erasing her words. "Never mind. Of course, we can go out to lunch. Sounds lovely, darlin'."

"Miss Smythe! Miss Smythe!" A very skinny man with flour in his hair came through a door from the back room. He was wearing an apron, which he wiped his hands on, and he was smiling, like nothing gave him more pleasure than seeing Lucy Smythe in his shop.

"Mr. Frankenberry, I'm so happy to see you," she said, putting her hand out over the counter, as if she were a duchess. He took her hand and brought it to his lips.

I mouthed, "Mr. Frankenberry?" to Bridget, and she shrugged, never taking her eyes off the taster cakes.

"It's almost the big day," Mr. Frankenberry announced, happily.

"Yes, it is. I'm coming to check on the rehearsal dinner cake." Lucy's voice dripped southern drawl, and she was completely calm, like she was pleased to see her rehearsal dinner wedding cake but not at all anxious about it. She could have given lessons on bridal etiquette. She was quintessential class.

"Of course. Right this way. I have it in a special room for my most special bride."

Lucy turned around to Bridget and me and beamed. "I'm a bride."

I gave her a hug. "I know. A beautiful bride with a beautiful cake." Her happiness was infectious, and I started to get excited about her wedding, too. Maybe her over-the-top wedding was just an outward sign of her happiness. Suddenly, I was glad she was doing it up big. Why shouldn't she have the best?

We followed the baker through the back room and into another, ice-cold, small room. Lucy's cake was sitting on a stainless steel table. The three of us gasped in unison when we saw it. We were shocked. Maybe even aghast. There was an ominous pause, where I could have sworn Lucy was revving up her outrage.

Something had gone terribly wrong with the cake. Terribly wrong.

"What the devil did you do to me?" Lucy demanded, her voice remaining calm.

"Don't you love it?" Mr. Frankenberry gushed, showing off the cake, like he was presenting on the *Price is Right*.

"What's your definition of love?" Lucy demanded. Her calm bride self was being sorely tested, and I worried for the restrained Eisenhower in her. Ditto the controlled Martha Stewart.

"I can assure you that it's one of a kind," the baker said.

It had to be a one of a kind. I couldn't figure out how there could be two cakes like this.

"It's very tall," I said, diplomatically. It was tall. About four feet tall. But that wasn't the problem with the cake.

"It's empowering," Bridget said. "I mean, sort of."

Lucy's face had turned bright red, despite the cold room. She took a deep, calming breath and ran a hand over her coat, like she was smoothing out wrinkles. "Gladie, what do you really think of this cake? Give us your honest opinion. I'm sure Mr. Frankenberry is curious."

"Well…"

"It could be used in eighth grade health class," Bridget suggested.

Lucy nodded and gave a pointed look at the baker. "It could be used in eighth grade health class," she repeated, nodding her head with each word.

"I thought it was for a rehearsal dinner," the baker asked, confused.

"A rehearsal dinner," Lucy said. "An elegant, upscale rehearsal dinner. A dinner for my friends to come celebrate with me. Did you think the cake was for a porn convention rehearsal dinner?"

She was still calm, but her voice was pinched. When she didn't get an answer from the baker, she slammed her hand down hard on the table. "It's a vagina!" she yelled. "It's a vagina cake! You made me a vagina cake for my wedding!"

It was a vagina cake. Half of it was a normal white wedding cake fit for a royal wedding, but the other half was carved out in the shape of an anatomically correct vagina.

"It's not a-a-a-what you said," the baker stammered. His face was bright red, now, too. "It's a geode. A beautiful, geode. You told me that your wedding is celebrating Cannes and its environs. This is an ode to nature. It's a custom made, one of a kind masterpiece."

It was an ode to nature all right.

Lucy marched around the table and grabbed a fistful of the baker's apron. She pulled him close, and with a voice low and deep like John Wayne, she threatened his life.

Bridezilla had awakened.

CHAPTER 2

Surprise! Probably the scariest word in the English language. Surprises are rarely good things, dolly. That's why I'm lucky because I don't get a lot of surprises. Most of the time, I see them coming before they arrive, and that gives me some time to prepare for them. But sometimes I'm surprised, and your matches are going to have plenty of surprises, bubeleh. Plenty! He shows up at the restaurant with a pet monkey. She shares a bedroom with her forty-year old brother. He's a meshugana who believes that he's Jon Snow in Game of Thrones. She's a mieskeit who likes to pick her nose at dinner. My matches have been surprised by all of these things. Nobody's perfect, but some surprises are deal-breakers. When preparing isn't enough, do damage control. But if you can't get the monkey away from the shlimazel and Plan A is giving you bupkes, go for Plan B. That's right. Run away.

*Lesson 22, Matchmaking advice from your
Grandma Zelda*

"Vagina!" Lucy screamed. "Vagina cake!"

Bridget clutched my arm in fear. Lucy was a terrifying sight. Her eyes were as big as saucers, and her body vibrated with fury. I had never seen Lucy blow her cool to this extent. She was the most put together woman I had ever met. But now she was out of her mind furious. Her rehearsal cake was a vagina, and boy, that pissed her off.

"Geode cake," Mr. Frankenberry countered in barely a croak. "Geode. Beautiful. Geode."

"It's not a geode! It's a vagina cake! I can't serve a vagina cake at my rehearsal dinner!"

She was right. It was totally a vagina cake. Anybody who had ever seen a vagina would have recognized it, immediately. And I was pretty sure everyone at the rehearsal dinner would have already seen a vagina somewhere. The cake could have been a sculpture in a gynecologist's office. The centerpiece at a Playboy convention. It was all vagina.

Vagina. Vagina. Vagina.

For the first time, I didn't want to eat cake.

"It cost twelve-thousand-dollars," Bridget whispered

in my ear.

"For a cake?" I whispered back, horrified. An Entenmann's chocolate cake was only $4.99 at Walleys. Lucy could have gotten an Entenmann's and had enough left over to buy twenty-four-hundred more Entenmann's. Twenty-four-hundred Entenmann's sounded like the world's best wedding to me.

Now I wanted an Entenmann's cake real bad.

Bridget nodded. "Twelve-thousand-dollars for a vagina cake."

"What are you going to do? What are you going to do?" Lucy screeched, still holding the baker by his apron. He blinked fast. Otherwise, he seemed nonplussed by not only the hysterical bride, but also the fact that he had unintentionally created edible female genitalia for the nuptials of probably his wealthiest client. Lucy didn't react well to Mr. Frankenberry's lack of reaction. Her face was purple, and she huffed and puffed like a locomotive preparing to climb a mountain.

"She's going to blow," I breathed. "Somebody call 911."

Bridget covered her belly with her hands. "Don't watch, Vladimir. Violence isn't a way to resolve conflict."

Lucy didn't agree. She dropped the baker and dove

her beautiful hands into the vagina cake. "Vagina!" she yelled, again, over and over, while she ripped it into pieces and threw them at Mr. Frankenberry.

It was sort of enthralling watching another person have a complete breakdown over a vagina cake, but I quickly remembered that this person was one of my best friends, and it was my responsibility as her maid of honor to make sure that she didn't wind up in jail or the funny farm before she walked down the aisle.

That's why I tackled Lucy, throwing my arms around her. She was harder to take down than one would think for a delicate southern belle. She was like a Scarlett O'Hara version of the Incredible Hulk. Her rage knew no bounds. At least it didn't know the bounds of best friends because she fought against my hold. Trying to get me loose, she pelted me with cake and shoved a grapefruit-sized piece of vagina cake up my nose. I realized that she was blind with rage, and it wasn't personal. I had gotten in between her and killing the man who made her a vagina cake for her rehearsal dinner, so I had to be taken down.

We circled around, my arms clamped around her middle. She shoved more cake in my face. Around and around we went, bumping into the stainless steel table. We were like female wrestlers who had no idea how to wrestle. I was having trouble breathing with the cake up my nose and I was more or less blind from the fondant in my eyes.

Wow, this maid of honor thing had really taken a turn for the worse. I was gasping for air, but all I was getting was frosting. I didn't want to die that way…murdered by vagina cake. Somehow, I had to wake Lucy up from her bridal freakout.

I coughed and sputtered and tried to catch my breath. "Stop, Lucy," I said, sounding like I had a rip-roaring head cold. "If you get arrested, I don't have enough money to bail you out. And don't forget there's no caviar facials or Hermes Egyptian cotton sheets in jail."

It was a sobering reminder for her. Lucy enjoyed her creature comforts. She blinked a few times, as if she was trying to focus. Finally, she seemed to recognize me. She calmed down a little and stopped fighting me. I kept my arms around her, just in case she went for a second go around.

"I think I'm okay now, darlin'," she said. "I was just a little out of sorts because Mr. Frankenberry ruined my life. Are you all right, Gladie?"

"I'm fine," I lied, hacking up some frosting.

"At least it was just for the rehearsal dinner, Lucy. Maybe he has time to make a new cake. Something not so medical," Bridget suggested.

Lucy physically relaxed and I let go of her. She pointed her cake-covered finger at the baker. "Can you do that?"

He smiled magnanimously, as if he was the wizard of perfect, non-vagina cakes. "Of course. So, no geode cake?"

Lucy lunged for him, but I caught her in time, clasping my hands around her again. "No geode cake! No geode cake!" I yelled. "Just make it like you did the rest of the cake without the you-know-what."

He backed up into the corner of the room. "I can do that."

"He can do that," I repeated.

"He can do it," Lucy said as she turned on her heel and walked out of the room. I took a breath trying to calm my heart, which was beating like a hummingbird's.

"Gee, cake is a tough business," Bridget commented, staring at the remains of the vagina cake.

"You have no idea," Mr. Frankenberry said.

Bridget handed me a Kleenex and I blew my nose, but the cake was wedged up there real good. I would have cake boogers for days, and I could only breathe through my mouth. I grabbed some napkins and tried to de-cake the rest of me. I had icing in my hair, and Spencer's cashmere sweater was ruined.

Being a maid of honor was a bitch.

Bridget and I found Lucy outside in front of the bakery. Somehow, Lucy had cleaned off all trace of the vagina cake from herself and was her normal, put-together southern belle self, again. Not a fleck of cake anywhere on her.

"Well, we can scratch that off our to do list," Lucy said.

She was outwardly calm, but I didn't think I should poke the tiger and ask to go get lattes.

"My rehearsal dinner is tomorrow and that Yankee made me a vagina cake," she said with a smile, but also a slight tinge of panic in her voice, as she towered over me in her heels. Her breath smelled sweet and fresh, as if she brushed her teeth with gardenias. If she was mentioning Yankees, I figured it was bad. "So much to do. So much to do," she added, as if she was speaking to herself. She stepped off the curb and beeped open her Mercedes.

Lucy Smythe was getting married and it was some serious shit.

I took my seat in the Mercedes as Lucy started it up and opened the roof. "I didn't know it was a convertible," I said.

"Hard top," she explained. She took a deep breath and drummed her fingers on the steering wheel. "I want to apologize for what happened in there. I had promised myself that I would enjoy the wedding process and not become a bridezilla."

She was the sweet, caring Lucy that I had always known. The wrestling match was forgotten, even though I still had cake up my nose. I gave her a one-armed hug. "Consider it forgotten. I would have done the same thing."

Mollified, she smiled and adjusted her fur hat on her head. She put the car into drive, but as she started to pull away from the curb, she had to slam on her brakes to avoid running over a pack of dogs. It was the wild Chihuahuas. They ran by fast, their little nails click-clacking on the pavement. They yapped at us as they passed and the message was clear: They weren't going to take crap from anyone. They were like a gang from West Side Story, almost dancing as they ran, with more than one of them wearing a ribbon and jingly bell around their necks.

"Holy shit, there they are," I said. "I thought it was a joke."

"Wow, those little guys get around," Bridget said.

"I've never heard of a pack of wild chihuahuas," I said, watching them run down the street. They had tiny little legs, but they were moving at a breakneck pace.

"I heard the original ones came into town when Paris

Hilton had a girls weekend here a couple years back," Bridget explained. "Each of her friends had carried one in their purses, but the dogs hopped out while they visited the apple orchards. I guess they bred, and the rest is history."

"Gosh," I said. "Just like *Jurassic Park*."

"I love this crazy town," Lucy said.

We sat in the car a moment, while we watched the pack of celebrity dogs run down the street. A minute later there was the sound of a siren and a cop car drove by, chasing the dogs.

"Look at that," Bridget said. "The dogs took a shortcut under the fence next to the pharmacy. How clever."

"Do you think other towns have packs of wild Chihuahuas?" I asked.

"I think this sort of thing stops at our border," Bridget said, thoughtfully.

"I feel much better now," Lucy said, once the dogs and the cops had passed. She made a big U-turn and pressed on the gas hard. "Oh, no. Look at the time. I have to hurry home to get my hair done," she explained.

She drove like a bat out of hell toward her house, passing other cars and narrowly missing a couple tourists as they crossed the street.

It was cold, but it was sunny, and even though Lucy was driving like she was the pace car at Nascar, it was a pleasure to ride with the car top down. I tugged my coat collar tight and enjoyed the ride.

Lucy lived outside of the Historic District in a large, white modern house made with lots of glass and chrome. It looked like it could have been Jennifer Aniston's house or Iron Man's. Someone with lots of money. It had a series of balconies, and one of them had a large hot tub on it. If I lived there, I might never leave.

She parked the Mercedes in the garage and hopped out. We went inside and walked upstairs to the main floor of the house. Everything was designer and decorated, the complete opposite of my grandmother's lived-in home.

Lucy whipped off her coat and hat and threw them on her white couch. She checked her watch. "She's supposed to be here," she said, tapping her foot and looking at her watch again. "I'm getting my hair done. Uncle Harry is going to take one look at me and... what does Zelda say, Gladie?"

"Plotz."

She pointed at me. "That's right. He's going to plotz."

The doorbell rang, and Lucy jumped in surprise.

"That's her. That's her," she exclaimed, hopping on

her heels as she ran for the front door.

"Is Bird working again? Bridget asked me. Bird Gonzalez owned the town's hair salon, and she was an amazing hairdresser, but a few weeks ago she had had some emotional problems, due to an unwise diet.

"She's still recovering, as far as I know," I said. "She hasn't come around to the house. My grandmother says one more week without her and she's going to color her hair from a box."

My grandmother had never colored her hair from a box. Bird had been giving Grandma weekly house calls for forever and, before that, it was someone else. I, on the other hand, was waiting for a Groupon so I could afford to get my hair cut.

Lucy returned with three women. They each carried a small suitcase, and they were dressed entirely in black. Their hair was slicked back and tied in ponytails. They looked like they had popped out of an eighties music video.

"This is Katia and her assistants," Lucy said, clapping her hands together. "They drove in from Los Angeles. They bumped Jennifer Lawrence to come here and do my hair."

I couldn't imagine what it had to cost to bump Jennifer Lawrence and have a team from Hollywood come hundreds of miles to do her hair. Probably more than

Walley's entire stock of Entenmann's. Lucy gestured toward her bedroom for them to set up. As they filed past, Lucy took Bridget's and my hands in hers.

Her face was bright with the excitement of a soon-to-be-bride. "Isn't this fun? Aren't we having fun? Wait until you see my hair. I'm getting it dyed to match my dress." She did a little jump in the air. "My wedding is going to be fabulous. And I haven't forgotten you two. I've kept my whole evening free tonight for the bachelorette party. I can't wait to see what you've planned for me."

She dropped our hands and skipped toward her bedroom to get her hair done.

Bridget and I exchanged looks, and it was clear that she hadn't thought about a bachelorette party any more than I had. "Bachelorette party? I am the world's worst friend," I breathed. I had been so caught up in my new relationship with Spencer that I hadn't given Lucy's wedding much thought. Since she was such a competent businesswoman and seemed to know exactly what she wanted for her wedding, it never dawned on me to ask her what help she wanted. My only attitude was to do whatever she asked me to do.

I figured that she would tell me where to stand, and I would stand there.

I sucked.

"*I'm* the world's worst friend," Bridget corrected. "Even though I don't believe in society's dictates about a woman being required to devote herself to domestic imprisonment merely to participate in sexual monogamy, I should have been more supportive of Lucy's desires to be married."

"Is the bachelorette party where we sit in a circle, play stupid games, and give her gifts?" I asked.

"Maybe? It's either that or the one where we get drunk."

I was all for getting drunk. It sounded easier than sitting in a circle, playing games. "We didn't give her a bridal shower, either. Were we supposed to do that?"

"I don't know because I don't believe in marriage," Bridget said. "Getting drunk sounds good though, but I can't get drunk for another four months."

"I'll take one for the team and drink your share, too," I said. "We can do this. We've got a couple hours before the bachelorette party. How hard can it be to plan one?"

Bridget's eyes grew wide with excitement. "Male strippers!" she announced, sticking her finger up in the air, like she had discovered electricity. "We'll want a bunch of those. Maybe we could grease them down. I think I'd like that." She stared off into space with a huge smile planted on her face, as if she was imagining herself greasing down a male stripper or two.

"That sounds good," I said and wondered how much it cost to grease down strippers.

"I need something cold to drink and something to eat," Bridget said, suddenly snapping out of her stripper reverie. "It takes a lot to handle all of these pregnancy hormones. It's like I'm running on high octane, but I'm only an electric golf cart. All that gas with nothing to use it for."

I put my arm around her shoulders. "Let's raid Lucy's kitchen while she's dying her hair to match her dress."

Bridget and I tackled the refrigerator first. It was a giant, double-sized one with a glass door, and it stood next to its twin freezer. The kitchen looked like it should be on a show on the Food Network or at least belong to the Queen of England.

"Lucy's really good at marketing," I said, marveling at her eight-burner stove.

"She has two warming ovens," Bridget commented in awe. "That's a lot to keep warm. Oh, and look at her wine."

There was a small refrigerator filled with wine bottles, tucked in next to a mystery appliance that we couldn't figure out. The rest of Lucy's house was just as fancy as the kitchen. Her bedroom looked like a modern version of Marie

Antoinette's, and her closet was three times the size of my bedroom. It would be hard to give up the house, but I couldn't imagine the house she was going to build with Uncle Harry. It would probably be like Hearst Castle.

I opened the fridge and took out a rotisserie chicken, a tub of potato salad, a tomato, mayonnaise, and a head of lettuce. Bridget found a loaf of bread in the cabinet next to a bag of chips, which she took out too.

While Bridget sat at the kitchen island, I made sandwiches, laying them out on paper towels. "I'm sure Zelda could put together a bachelorette party in no time," Bridget said, grabbing a chip.

I wasn't so sure. Grandma was the before-the-wedding person, not the actual wedding person, but she did know everyone in town, so that would make it easier to organize.

"Maybe we could just kidnap Lucy and drive her to Vegas," I said, hopefully.

"Too far. We wouldn't get back in time for the rehearsal dinner. Oh! There's a new casino just east of Cannes. We could do that. I think they might even have a male stripper show. That would be easy. Zelda could do the invites and everyone could meet us there. Booze, games, entertainment."

It was a great idea. Easy. I loved easy. "You're a genius."

"And while we're there, I could protest the spending of money on gambling instead of giving charity to the less fortunate, like the women's shelter. I have a new sandwich board that I'm itching to try out."

"Maybe not," I said.

"Okay. The sandwich board probably doesn't fit me, anyway."

I finished making the sandwiches and sat next to Bridget at the island. We got halfway through our food when Lucy floated in, like a Southern angel in peach organza. Her hair had been dyed to match her peach dress and curled into tight ringlets, just like Scarlett, tied back with a peach bow.

"You look..." I started.

"Like a goddess!" she finished, spinning around. "I've never felt so beautiful in my life."

"I've never seen that color hair," Bridget said. Her mouth was open, revealing a half-masticated bite of sandwich.

"Princess Peach," Lucy announced. "Isn't it dreamy?"

Yes. I did kind of feel like I was dreaming. Her hair was an unnatural color, but it did match her dress. She was the princess in peach. Glowing, pretty, and classy.

And peach.

"Dreamy," I said, and Bridget nodded, swallowing down her bite of sandwich with a loud gulp.

The hairdressers came into the kitchen, all packed up and ready to go. "New technique," Katia said, pointing at Lucy's hair. "Very fast. Make you not look so old."

Lucy's smile faltered. "Yes, well…"

"Good product from home country," Katia continued. "Can't use in America."

"You can't?" Bridget asked.

"Fucking America. Fucking EPA," one of Katia's assistants said and spit.

Lucy handed the head cosmetologist a thick roll of dollars and walked the beauty team to the front door. When she returned, I gave her a sandwich that I had made for her and went back to eating mine.

"Yum," she said, taking a bite. I couldn't cook anything, but I made a mean sandwich.

"Sorry again about earlier," Lucy said, sitting on a stool across from me. "I had a little bridezilla attack, but it's over now."

"You weren't a bridezilla. You had an understandable reaction to the cake."

Lucy closed her eyes and took a deep breath, seeming to exhale the memory of the cake out of her system. "Well, now I'm going to roll with the punches. I'm the Zen bride. I'm one with the process. And check out my do. Isn't it fabulous?"

She ran a hand over her curls before resting it on the counter next to her plate. I stared at her hand in horror. A thick, peach ringlet was woven around her fingers, removed from the root like it had dissolved when she ran her hand over her head.

Lucy was oblivious that she now had a nickel-sized bald spot on her head. She was talking about the peach flower arrangements at her rehearsal dinner and her surprise peach cocktail that she was going to serve. She was gesturing with her left hand, completely unaware that her hair was under her right hand.

But it was only a matter of time—and not a lot of time—before she was aware.

I wanted to run very far away. Somewhere with a bomb shelter. I mean, how much could a bride take? Vagina cake was one thing, but going bald a few days before her wedding was another.

Surreptitiously, I looked at Bridget. She had noticed the hair, too, and she was waiting for Lucy to blow, holding her sandwich halfway between her plate and her mouth. Her hoot owl glasses made her eyes look huge, and she wasn't blinking.

"Okay. Okay, I'll tell you," Lucy continued, happy as a clam. "Lucy-tail. That's the name of the special drink. Lucy-tail. And you'll never guess this. Never in a million years. But they're going to be served in ostrich eggshells. Isn't that fabulous?"

She leaned forward, waiting for me to agree that ostrich eggshells were fabulous. I smiled as much as I could, considering that I knew that she was about to discover that she was missing a clump of hair, and nodded slowly.

Then, it happened.

Lucy touched her head again, bouncing her perfect, peach curls, and this time a bunch of them fell off her head *plop!* onto her plate next to her mound of untouched potato chips.

Lucy's smile dropped, and she looked down at her plate. Her forehead transformed into an array of thick wrinkles, and she cocked her head to the side, as if she was trying to figure out why there was a bunch of peach hair on her plate.

The moment she recognized the hair as her own was pretty obvious. Her eyes grew larger than Bridget's. Her mouth dropped open, but no words came out. Her hand rose in the air on its way to her head.

"It's not that bad," I croaked. "It can be fixed. It can..." I ran out of lies. It was a pretty desperate situation. Bridget stuffed her sandwich in her mouth, presumably so she couldn't answer any questions about Lucy's balding problem.

Lucy touched her head and lowered her hand with more ringlets in it. "Ohhhh..." she started like she was a tornado warning system.

"It's not that bad!" I shouted, but she was louder than I was. She touched her head, feeling the bald spots, which were now more numerous than her non-bald spots.

"Ohhhh..." she continued with impressive breath control.

Lucy ran to her bedroom, and Bridget and I followed. We found her in her bathroom, looking at her head in a three-way mirror.

"I'm... I'm..." she said.

Bald. That was the word she was looking for. Actually, she wasn't totally bald. She still had a few long, peach ringlets here and there over her scalp. That must have been the superhuman hair, able to resist the toxic power of

Katia's EPA-defying secret sauce. The rest was bald.

"It'll grow back," Bridget said. A few months ago, Bridget's hair was more or less burned off, forcing her to cut her hair into a short bob, which had since grown back. But she had never been like this. Bald.

Lucy gave her a death stare, like she was a DMV lady, and Bridget had forgotten to bring her correct paperwork. Then, Lucy's face relaxed, and she slumped onto a chair. Her shoulders went up and down, and there was a strange sound coming out of her.

"Are you all right?" I asked.

"Are you crying or laughing?" Bridget asked Lucy.

"I'm bald," she said pointing to her reflection in the mirror. "The crazy town got me. I'm bald."

Bridget turned toward me. "She's laughing, I think. But maybe you should get the Xanax. You have any Xanax, Lucy?"

But Lucy wasn't listening. She was laughing, hysterically. After a few minutes, she finally caught her breath and put her hands up. "Okay. Okay. I give up. It was my turn, I guess."

She had a point. Usually, the shit hit my fan, not hers. And Bridget's car was eaten by a bear, so baldness was just par for the course.

"Wow, weddings are tough," Bridget noted.

"At least Jennifer Lawrence dodged a bullet," I said.

Lucy wiped her eyes, which had gotten teary from laughing. "I've been thinking about it, and Grace Kelly wore a pearl-embroidered headpiece," Lucy said after a moment. "I'd look damned good in a pearl-embroidered headpiece."

"Of course you would."

Lucy sat up, making her remaining peach ringlets boing into place. "I'm not a bridezilla."

"No one said you were."

"I mean, I'm bald."

"Right?"

"And a vagina cake. I mean, really?"

"Exactly."

"I'm a strong southern woman," she said in her *Gone With the Wind* drawl. "I don't need hair to get married. There's no rule about needing hair. I'll get a pearl-embroidered headpiece. In fact, I'll get two. Three. I'll be drop dead gorgeous."

"Drop dead."

She arched an eyebrow. "Excuse me?"

"I mean, drop dead gorgeous."

"Now what?" she asked.

I thought quickly. "Bridget and I are surprising you. We're going to your bachelorette party, and it's going to be fabulous."

"Thank God. I need to get drunk and be among friends. Celebrate me, world. Celebrate me!"

CHAPTER 3

Two things are always true about matches. One: At some point, they're going to fart. Two: They have secrets. I don't mind matches having secrets, but if they're determined to keep them, they have to be aware that at some point those secrets are going to bite them in the ass. So, ask your matches if they have any secrets that could derail their happiness. Explain to them that a secret is like sweeping crumbs under a rug. The crumbs might stay there, but they'll attract bugs. Nobody likes bugs, bubeleh. Nobody.

Lesson 43, Matchmaking advice from your
Grandma Zelda

"Tell me the truth," Lucy urged, as she drove us to my grandmother's house.

"It looks beautiful," I lied. I was getting tired of lying.

Being a maid of honor was exhausting. It was all lies, lies, lies. If I was Pinocchio, my nose would be twelve-feet long. I was two lies away from being elected president.

"Are you sure?" she asked, checking herself out in the rearview window. The car swerved, as she studied her reflection. She was wearing a Hermes scarf, wrapped over her head and around her neck. She had plucked one of her last peach ringlets out of the scarf to dangle over the side of her face, but a strip of bald scalp was visible, no matter how she adjusted the scarf.

"Gorgeous," I assured her.

"Men don't care if they have hair," Bridget said from the back seat. "Why should women care?"

"Men care if they have hair," I said and turned my head to shoot her a *shut up* death stare.

"But I look like I have hair, right?" Lucy said.

"Of course," I said.

"It just looks like I've decided to wear a beautiful scarf?" she asked.

"Absolutely." The lying was wearing me out.

"When does the drinking start?" Bridget asked.

I hoped it would start soon. Since we were lying

about the planning of her bachelorette party, we were winging it. We were going to run home for me to change and to secretly tell Grandma to gather up the troops to meet us at the casino. Then, we were going to head out of town to get plastered until Lucy wouldn't care if she was bald or not. Hopefully, she would never find out that we hadn't thought to throw her a party until she reminded us.

"What the dickens?" Lucy asked, still looking in the rearview mirror. "The fuzz is after us, girls."

There was a police siren, and Lucy pulled over to the side. The siren stopped. I watched through the side mirror as Spencer hopped out of his car behind us and walked toward us. I watched him saunter and my heart sped up. He caught my reflection in the mirror and smirked. Yowza was he good-looking. He seemed to have been getting more handsome every day since we sealed the deal. Was that possible? Perhaps he had a sexy superpower.

His arms bulged in his tailored suit, as he buttoned his jacket. Lucy had put the top up so that her scarf wouldn't get blown off, and now, Spencer kneeled down at my door and knocked on my window. I opened it.

He arched an eyebrow, as his eyes gave me the once-over. "I wanted to let you know that I made a reservation at six for us for dinner. The dessert will come later, of course."

Spencer reached out and touched my cheek, sending

shivers through my body but spreading heat to my core. "That sounds lovely," I breathed.

He took my hand and brought it to his lips, kissing it gently. "I'll pick you up at five-forty-five, then. And Pinky, wear something skimpy."

"Skimpy," I breathed and then giggled.

"Gladie's going to get drunk tonight," Bridget announced from the back seat. "She can't go out with you."

"Drunk?" Spencer asked.

"My bachelorette party, darlin'," Lucy said. "They're going to celebrate me before my nuptials."

"We can move dessert to another night," I offered Spencer.

"Oh." He was obviously disappointed, which thrilled me. Spencer blinked. "Where the hell did your hair go? Is that some kind of new fashion?"

Lucy's mouth dropped open, and her hands flew to her head, feverishly adjusting the scarf. "Gladie, you swore to me that it wasn't noticeable."

"He's joking," I lied. "Tell her you're joking." I reached out and pinched him as hard as I could to make my point. He slapped my hand away and yelped in pain.

"What was that for?" he demanded, and I pinched him, again, even harder this time.

"Okay! Okay! Sorry, Lucy. I was joking. You look resplendent."

I didn't know what resplendent meant, but Lucy seemed happier. "I have to pee," Bridget announced. "I'm pregnant, you know."

"I guess that's goodbye?" Spencer asked me.

I shrugged. "Sorry."

His eyes searched mine, and I shivered. "Not as sorry as I am, Pinky." He wagged his finger at me. "No more trouble."

And that was goodbye. Spencer gave me a quick kiss with tongue, and Lucy peeled away from the curb, the tires squealing. When we got to my grandmother's house, I dressed as quickly as I could into a skirt, blouse, and heels. Lucy was still dressed in her peach dress, and Bridget was wearing a blue maternity dress and flats.

While they waited for me in the parlor, I cornered Grandma in the kitchen and asked her to send over everyone to the casino who was close to Lucy. "Are you sure that's a good idea, dolly?" she asked. "Everyone?"

"I'm trying to be a good friend. I totally failed with

the bachelorette party. I didn't plan anything at all. I need bodies to make a good show."

"Well, if you insist," she said and placed a wad of bills in my hand. I looked at her, questioningly. "For the party," she explained. "Think of it as my gift. Give her a good party."

I hugged my grandmother. Then I met Bridget and Lucy in the parlor, and we left for the casino. To her credit, Lucy had put aside her hair drama and was ready to have fun. The casino had been built only five years before, cut into the hills outside of Cannes. It was a squat, vast wooden building with an attached hotel about ten stories tall. The sun was setting as we drove up to the valet stand. It was too early to start partying, but we didn't care. We needed some distraction on the double.

"You have a male stripper show, right?" Bridget asked the valet, as we got out of the car.

"The Big Postal Packages show. That's right, ma'am," he said.

"Oh, yes. They're all retired mailmen. I forgot about that," Bridget said.

I stood between my best friends and wrapped my arms around their waists. "Girls," I announced. "We're here to be rowdy, naughty, and generally disgusting. Are you ready?"

"I'm ready," Bridget said.

"In my head, I'm already on my third drink," Lucy said.

It didn't take long for Lucy to get on her actual third drink. We walked into the first cocktail lounge that we found. It was a round bar with multi-colored chairs that matched the carpet. Dimly lit, there were candles at the center of each table. The lounge was surrounded by rows and rows of slot machines. Even though it was four-thirty on a Wednesday, the casino was packed with gamblers, and at least half of them had gotten a big head start in getting sloshed.

Lucy and I ordered dirty martinis, and Bridget ordered a virgin piña colada. I was still working on my first drink when Lucy ordered her third, and the cocktail waitress Peggy kept us in Chex Mix and salted peanuts. We found out that the Big Postal Packages were stripping at eight, which gave us plenty of time to hit the buffet before we got an eyeful of their big packages.

"I love you," Lucy gushed, lifting her glass in a toast and spilling half of her drink. "I love Uncle Harry more, but I love you both heaps and loads!"

She hopped up and started to dance the twist even

though the canned music coming out of the bar's speakers was a Celine Dion ballad.

"Go, girl!" a drunk man cheered Lucy on. He was wandering through the lounge, carrying a drink. Sixty-something, wearing pleated Dockers and a golf shirt with an intricate comb-over, he was a dead-ringer for Uncle Harry, except that he was six inches taller and he had a neck. Lucy continued to twist while Celine sang about heartbreak, and Lucy's martini sloshed all over the floor. The man threw a wad of bills onto our table. "I love a woman who can dance," he cried and added a *yahoo!* as punctuation. "Have a great time, ladies!"

It was the second time that day that I had been given a pile of money. It was like Christmas and the parting of the Red Sea and a winning lottery ticket all at the same time. "Capitalism is the flesh-eating bacteria of a healthy society," Bridget told the generous, drunk man.

"Excuse me?" he said.

"Flesh-eating bacteria," she said louder, pointing at the wad of cash.

"She said thank you," I explained, pushing her hand down gently and grabbing the cash. "She's from out of town."

The man shrugged and danced away to a slot machine. Lucy called over the waitress for another drink.

"This is great. This is great," she said, slapping my back, hard. "Friends. Booze. I'm getting married, you know."

"You're getting married," I said, toasting her. "You're going to be so happy."

Lucy gulped at her drink, slammed it down on the table, and wiped her mouth with the back of her hand. "I'm so happy. So happy." Her voice hitched, and she looked up at the glittery ceiling. "You know, my darlins', I never thought I would get married. I come from people—well, you don't want to hear about that—but I've worked hard to get to where I am."

"I think you're probably the best marketing person in the world," I said. Whatever that meant.

Lucy sniffed and wiped at her eye. "Shank you," she slurred. "Shank you, Gaddie. I've worked sho hard for sho many years. All on my own! She this dress? I bought this dress from hard work. She this scarf? I bought this scarf from hard work. She these breasts? Hard work! Lawd, don't they have air conditioning in this place? It's awfully hot in here. Hey, Peggy, can I get another?"

She lifted her empty glass in the air. It was probably time for the buffet so Lucy could dry out enough before the stripper show. If she had one more drink, I feared for the Big Postal Packages. Before I could ask for the check, we were interrupted by more bachelorette party guests. Thankfully,

Grandma had come through with three people to celebrate Lucy.

"Hello, Gladie. Hello, Bridget. Lucy, this is for you." Meryl, the blue-haired librarian handed Lucy what looked like a gift-wrapped mug. Meryl had shown up with Ruth Fletcher, the owner of Tea Time, and another woman who I didn't recognize. The woman waved to me.

"Hi, Gladie," she said.

I offered her my hand. "Hi, I'm Gladie."

She put her hands on her hips and looked at me askance. "It's me."

"Of course," I said, even though I had no idea who she was. Bridget kicked me hard under the table and swirled her eyes around in their sockets, like she was messaging me about something, but I had no idea what.

"Bird, is that you in there?" Lucy asked, leaning forward and slapping her elbows on the table. "Honey, you look like you rolled yourself in biscuit dough."

"Bird?" I asked, squinting. As long as I had known Bird, she was in perfect shape and striving to be in even better shape. Almost every month, she was on a new diet. Working as a hairdresser for twelve hours a day kept her firm and toned.

Until now.

I hadn't seen her in a few weeks since she had had a nervous breakdown, but whoa, she must have eaten everything in a ten-mile radius since then. She had ballooned up. She probably gained thirty pounds. At least. But I had insulted her by not recognizing her, and she was visibly hurt.

"Bird!" I exclaimed with my mouth upturned in a big smile, trying to minimize the damage. "I'm so drunk. So drunk. I wouldn't recognize my own mother because I'm so drunk. Really drunk. Drunk. Sloshed."

Bridget kicked me under the table, again, and I shut my mouth. The damage was done. Bird didn't buy my drunk excuse. She dropped her hands, and her face dropped, too, in total defeat and humiliation.

"Good one, Gladie," Ruth sneered and grabbed a seat, sitting down next to me. "I hear you're getting hitched, fancy girl," she said to Lucy. "I heard that you're getting the Bee Gees to perform at your wedding."

"The Bee Gees are dead," Lucy said. "Sho we're getting Beyoncé."

"Beyoncé? Beyoncé is going to be at your wedding?" I asked.

"I don't know who the hell that is," Ruth said. "But I hear that your wedding costs more than an aircraft carrier."

That sounded like a lot of money.

"You can't put a price tag on love," Lucy said and wiped at her eyes. "Where's the drinks?"

They ordered another round, and the drinks arrived quickly. "I was married once, but he died in a train accident," Meryl said, sipping her margarita.

Bridget's ears perked up. "Did he get hit by a train? Train conductors work under terrible conditions. I once chained myself to a train for two days so the conductor could get some rest."

"He didn't get hit by a train," Meryl said, focusing on the interior of her glass.

"He robbed a train, and when he jumped off afterward, he broke his neck," Ruth explained, downing a shot of tequila. "I was never married. You couldn't pay me to sign this over. You know what I mean?"

I had no idea what she meant.

"I've been married six times," Bird said, chewing a mouthful of peanuts. "Five men, six weddings. I like weddings, too, Lucy. During one wedding, I had a flock of flamingoes line the aisle where I walked to my groom. It was a better idea than it was in practice. But my colors were blush pink and hot pink. So, you know."

"Flamingoes," I said, nodding.

"Now, I'm too fat to get married," she said, chewing on more peanuts. "I'm fat, fat, fat. I've got fat everywhere. From my head to my toes. Fat. Do they have any chips? I could go for chips."

"There's a buffet. We're going there before the strippers," I said.

Bird's ears perked up. "Buffet sounds good."

"And the stripper show serves nachos and jalapeno poppers," Bridget added. She knew an awful lot about the stripper show.

"I like buffets and jalapeno poppers," Bird said, eating the rest of the peanuts.

"I guess Gladie will be the next to get married," Meryl said, effectively ending the conversation about food. Everyone looked at me, as if they were waiting for the announcement of my pending nuptials. But I didn't have any nuptials pending. In fact, I hadn't even thought about nuptials. I was only halfway comfortable at the idea of being in a committed relationship.

"Holy hell, Gladie, what's happening with your face?" Ruth asked.

"Nothing." I looked down at my drink.

"I was saying that Gladie will be next," Meryl continued. "Spencer is practically living with her. Zelda says he even gets his dry cleaning delivered there. I figure he's got to pop the question any second. Are you okay, Gladie? Your face is doing something. Maybe you're allergic to something."

"My face is fine," I said.

"It's the marriage thing," Ruth said. "She's freaking out about marrying the cop."

"Every woman in Cannes would kill to marry the cop," Bird said. "There's a half dozen women in this town ready to poison Gladie the first chance they get."

I put my drink down.

"Gladie, it looks like your nose is going to take flight," Ruth said. "You sucked your lips into your mouth, and your cheeks are doing the cha-cha."

I tried to relax my face, but they were right. I was having some kind of reaction. "Think happy thoughts," Bridget told me. "Think about being single. I mean, Spencer hasn't proposed, yet, so he probably doesn't even want to get married."

I relaxed, and my cheeks stopped dancing the cha-cha. Bridget was right. Spencer had never mentioned the "M" word to me. Just a couple weeks ago, he was still dating half of the women in Southern California, so he wasn't exactly a family kind of man. Not that I wasn't crazy about him, but the idea of marriage… I shuddered.

"She's getting color back in her face, and it's not doing that thing, anymore," Meryl commented. The others nodded after studying my face a moment. Thankfully, with my face back to normal, attention went back to Lucy and her Princess Diana-level wedding.

"This is a lovely time," Lucy gushed, completely blotto. "Lovely. I love getting married. Being with friends. Everyone is happy for me. Aren't weddings lovely? I'm so happy. Nothing could stop my happiness. Nothing!"

Occasionally, when people said things like this, my grandmother would spit. She said it was to ward against the evil eye. Unfortunately, as Lucy announced that nothing could stop her happiness, I didn't think about spitting. I had completely forgotten about the evil eye.

But the evil eye was on its way. Big time.

In this case, it went into effect almost immediately. Our little table of revelers were interrupted by two middle-aged people—a woman and a man. The woman had big hair and wore a hot pink suit and bright red lipstick that bled outside the lines of her lips. The man wore cutoff jean shorts and an *I Love Bacon* t-shirt, and he had stick straight hair that hung down to his chin in greasy strips.

"Looky here, Cletus," the woman said. "Sis done got herself hitched."

I followed her line of sight to Lucy's face, which had dropped in a mixture of dread, panic, shock, and dead soberness. Lucy had been sloshed a few seconds ago, but that was long gone.

"What the…" she started.

"Sissy, don't you look prettier than a hog at the county fair," Cletus gushed and marched to Lucy and gave her a bear hug.

"Wha-wha-wha are you doing here?" she asked.

"We came to visit," Cletus announced. "An old lady told us you're getting married and told us to get over here to celebrate. Does this mean you're not a hooker anymore?"

Everyone's mouth dropped in unison and all heads turned toward Lucy, including mine. Lucy's alcohol-infused red face had drained of color, and she pushed back on her scarf, revealing a large swathe of baldness and two long, peach ringlets.

"Not that we ever judged, sis," the woman in pink told Lucy. "You wanted to be a hooker, and that was fine with us because you were happy." She slapped the side of her head. "Did I say, hooker? I meant, 'call girl.' That's what you call it, right? I need to say it right or else you get pushed out of shape like a sweater washed with the jeans. Call. Girl."

Meryl rubbed her ear, as if she wasn't sure what she was hearing. But I was sure. Hooker. Call girl.

Finally, I knew what "marketing" meant.

The woman in pink gave Lucy a big hug, and the drunk man from before returned, drunker now and holding a sparkler. "How's the party goin'?" he asked, his voice booming over the canned music and stumbling over his own feet. He was drunk up to his eyeballs. He handed Lucy his sparkler. "Here you go, girl. Have fun."

The second that she took the sparkler, the drunk man passed out on the table with a thud, knocking over three drinks. Lucy flinched, lifting her arms up, and that's when the sparkler set one of her last ringlets and her Hermes scarf on fire.

CHAPTER 4

There's an expression -- I think Willard Scott said it on the Today Show—"Calm before the storm." So, your matches will know this expression and when it's calm, they'll think: "Yes, but it's the calm before the storm." In other words, they'll be nervous. It's your job to calm them down, dolly. Explain to them that there isn't always a storm after the calm. Sometimes it stays calm. But between you and me, usually it's just storm. Storm before the storm. Storm after the storm. Where's the calm? You'll be calm when you're dead. (But you might want to keep that nugget of information to yourself. Your matches have enough to worry about.)

Lesson 108, Matchmaking advice from your
Grandma Zelda

It had been a rough and wild ride during the past

forty hours. After the sparkler incident, the casino's fire alarm, and its very efficient sprinkler system, the paramedics were called in to help Lucy. Luckily, the sprinklers doused her head before it could cause any damage, but the paramedics took her to the hospital to get checked out anyway. Uncle Harry insisted that Lucy go to West Side Hospital, a private, all-cash outfit for the uber rich. I heard that they gave mani / pedis during surgery and for an added fee, a boob job with every hysterectomy.

But that was just rumor because I didn't go with Lucy to her high-class hospital. Spencer showed up at the casino along with the firefighters and three squad cars. He took one look at Lucy's bald head, the flooded casino, and my drenched clothes and said, "Are you kidding me?" and took me home, where he stripped me out of my wet clothes and made love to me for hours until we stopped to eat leftover lasagna in the kitchen because I had skipped the buffet and was starving.

The next day, Grandma's house was a beehive of activity. With the news of Lucy's marketing career-- which had nothing to do with marketing--sweeping through the town like wildfire, the townsfolk had invaded my grandmother's to get the scoop. There hadn't been this much excitement about one of our locals since George Clooney drove through town, got a flat tire on Main Street, and ate a slice of apple pie in a restaurant while the tire was getting fixed. That episode caused a riot and a stampede, and it looked like this time would be no different.

So, the house was jam packed with nosy neighbors. Grandma, as usual, was discreet. Whenever there was a question about Lucy's call girl job, my grandmother would turn the conversation to love, which didn't distract one busybody from their pursuit of juicy information.

And their pursuit of me. Since Lucy was in the hospital, they were trying to get the information out of her best friend. Of course, I knew nothing about her secret profession, but that didn't stop them from trying to squeeze out every detail from me.

That's why I was in hiding in my bedroom.

"Whatever you do, dolly," my grandmother told me in the morning before the rehearsal dinner. "don't go downstairs today. It'll be bad. I'll bring up food and water."

"I have a Men Aren't Really Pigs class to lead at noon," I told her. She patted my cheek and *tsk tsked*.

"Oh, bubeleh. If you go down there, there's an army of yentas who will tear you to pieces, trying to get information about Lucy. So, let them think that men are pigs for another day."

I rubbed my throat. I didn't want to be torn to pieces by gossip-needy women. But I did feel guilty about my professional life. I hadn't done one match all month, and since it was Valentine's Day month, there was a lot of pressure to get matches paired up. Grandma threw me a pointed look, which said that I was crazy not to take her advice. She was right. Grandma was always dead on with advice.

So, I stayed in my room all day, fielding calls from Lucy, who left the hospital after a few hours with a heavy dose of tranquilizers and a beaded headpiece that Uncle Harry helicoptered in for her from Los Angeles.

"I feel great!" she told me on the phone. "That hospital was better than The Red Door. They gave me a hot stones massage, a small nip / tuck, and they even polished my head. And Gladie," she added in a whisper into the phone. "They gave me some great drugs. It's like I'm a groupie at a Grateful Dead concert. I'm so high that I saw Teddy Roosevelt walk by my room. Teddy Roosevelt, Gladie."

With Lucy taken care of in her fancy hospital and me hiding from the throngs of yentas downstairs, I watched *Murder She Wrote* reruns in bed until it was time to get ready to go to the rehearsal dinner. Spencer and I got dressed together in my room.

"I don't understand what the rehearsal dinner is," Spencer complained, adjusting his tie in the mirror. He was wearing an Armani suit, which hugged him in all the right places. I wanted to hug him in all of the right places, too, but I was wrestling with my rehearsal dinner maid of honor dress that Lucy had picked out special for me. It was a peach organza ankle-length gown with a slit up the right front leg with patches of peach crocheted lace, covering my breasts. It wasn't horrible as maid of honor rehearsal dinner dresses went, and Lucy had given it to me as a gift, along with the maid of honor dress for the actual wedding. I slipped on the peach strappy sandals and stood three inches taller, coming up to Spencer's neck.

"You look interesting," he said, buttoning his blazer and eyeing me up and down.

"Thanks a lot. Is that your best boyfriend line?"

Spencer stepped toward me, wrapped his arm around my waist and pulled me tight against him, grinding his pelvis into me. "No, this is my best boyfriend line," he said, smirking and grinding.

"You are five years old."

"Five years old with ten minutes to spare before we have to go to the rehearsal dinner, whatever the hell that is." He arched an eyebrow, like he was asking me permission to fill the ten minutes the way he wanted. But I couldn't afford to mess up my hair. It had taken me forever to tame my curls into a semblance of an updo, and I didn't want to screw it up. I wished Bird would get over her nervous breakdown in a hurry. She could updo in only a few seconds.

"Sorry," I said. "I don't have time for your ten minutes and your boyfriend line. I have to get to this thing early to support Lucy. She's completely bald, now, and she's worried that some horrible tragedy is going to happen to ruin her event. I told her that a vagina cake and baldness was probably her allotment of tragedy for this wedding. But she's on edge."

Spencer nodded. "Harry told me that Lucy was chugging Ativan like it was M&M's." I stared at Spencer, unblinking. "Okay. Okay. You want M&M's now, right?" I nodded. "Fine. We'll stop at the Speedy Mart on our way."

The rehearsal dinner was on the banks of a picture-perfect lake in Cannes's mountains. An enormous peach-colored tent was set up next to a gorgeous wedding scene. Dozens of folding chairs were set up in rows on either side of a peach carpet, which led to a flower-laden canopy, where I assumed the rehearsal would take place. It was beautiful, and I wondered if all rehearsal dinners were like this. It was my first, and it almost made me want to get married.

Almost.

"I hate weddings. I hope there's booze," Spencer said,

parking in the makeshift parking lot, which was being managed by a couple of teenage boys dressed in white shirts and vests. There were portable heaters dotting the area, but it was still a cold day. "At least there's no snow on the ground. There they are. Put your smile on."

Lucy and Harry were standing near the canopy, ordering a bunch of people around. I put my smile on as well as the peach faux fur wrap that Lucy had gifted me to keep me warm in the February weather. Out of the car, Spencer put his hand on the small of my back and escorted me along the peach carpet to my friend.

"Hello, darlin'," she said, giving me air kisses. She was wearing a floor-length peach gown with a full corset and a peach headpiece that completely covered her bald head. "I'm so glad you're early. I've been trying to lasso these people, and…what was I saying?"

"Her pupils are fully dilated," Spencer whispered in my ear. "She's stoned out of her mind."

I was sort of relieved that Lucy was tranquilized for the rehearsal dinner. She had been through a lot lately and under a lot of stress, even though she had an army of wedding helpers. She might be stoned, but at least she was happy.

"You look beautiful," I told her, kissing her cheek. "This is some set up."

"Just a little gathering," she said. "Fifty people. Max. My sister and brother are coming," she added, rolling her bloodshot eyes. A van rolled up near the tent with *Happily Ever After Bakery* written in big, bold letters on its side. "Finally. Let's go check out that cake Gladie and see if it's a ball sack or whatever this time," she said taking a step. Her ankle wobbled on her high heel, but she managed to right herself. "You know, darlin', I feel pretty good. Like I'm out hunting deer and a bear lands in my lap. I'm gonna shoot that bear in the head and put it up on my wall, darlin'," she announced, making a shooting gesture with her hands.

"That sounds good?" I said, like a question. I took her arm, helping her to walk to the tent where the bakery deliverymen were carrying the rehearsal dinner cake. They were double-stepping it, like they were in a hurry, and a bad feeling crept up my spine.

As we walked away, Spencer slapped Harry on his back, while Harry lit up a cigar. "Well, the ball and chain, right?" Spencer said.

"Your turn next," Harry said, blowing out smoke.

"Ha! Yeah, right," I heard Spencer say, and then Lucy and I were too far away for me to make out what he said next. My heart was pounding in my chest, and I willed it to calm down. All the talk of marriage was freaking me out. No way was I ready to settle down and cook and clean for a living.

That wasn't my style. My style was more like running away after a couple weeks. I turned my head and stole a glance at Spencer. He was laughing with Uncle Harry, and he looked worry-free. Happy. And he was hotter than lava in his suit. It dawned on me that he was all mine. At least for now.

"Harry bought me sixteen headpieces in assorted colors," Lucy told me, as we walked to the tent. "He's my honeybunch. He told me that he loves me even though my head is tore slap up, and the town says I'm a whore."

"They don't say that," I said, but I was dying to ask her a million questions about her being a whore. How much of a whore was she? How long had she been a whore? What did it mean exactly to be a whore?

The bakers had put the cake down on the center table in the tent, and they ran back to the van, as if they were going for gold at the Olympics. Since Lucy was drugged, I allowed myself one question about her professional career. "So, when you said you were in marketing…" I began.

She wagged her finger at me, like she was teaching me something. "Gladie, there ain't a marketer in the world who has a Hartmann ruby-encrusted toilet roll holder."

She had a point. Lucy had money up the ring-ding. "So, you must be really good in bed," I dared.

Lucy stopped and gave me a pointed look. "I'm spectac-u-lar." She dragged out each syllable, locking eyes with me, and I believed her. It was one of very few jobs that I had never tried. But I wasn't sure a Hartmann ruby-encrusted toilet roll holder was worth doing it.

I had so many other questions, like if Lucy met Uncle Harry on the job and what he thought about her past profession. But Lucy's rehearsal dinner wasn't the place to ask the questions. I would have to get Lucy a lot drunker first.

"Well, bless his heart," Lucy said, as we reached the table with the cake. Like the vagina cake, this cake was a tall, white tower of confection. True to the baker's word, there was no genitalia. But even though it wasn't a porn cake, the baker had definitely taken revenge on Lucy for being so demanding and for having a breakdown in his bakery.

Lucy and I stared at the cake a moment, taking it all in. The baker had made a cake into an exact representation of Joseph Stalin down to his mustache and eyebrows. Thankfully, Lucy was higher than a kite.

"What the hell is that, sis?" Lucy's brother Cletus asked, coming up behind us and slapping her back with a loud clack.

"It's Stalin," she said.

He leaned over and studied the cake. "Looks like cousin Bubba," he said. "Where's the open bar?"

He was wearing a suit that was two sizes too big, as if he had borrowed it. He had a fresh bowl haircut, and he looked pleased as punch. His head turned from side to side, as he searched for the open bar. Lucy grabbed his arm. "Hold on, Cletus. Do you have the ring?"

"Right here," he said, patting his crotch.

"What?" she asked, looking at his crotch.

"There's the bar," he announced happily and skipped toward it.

Lucy's sister appeared in a hot pink suit and lace gloves. "You put Bubba on the cake?" she asked Lucy. "That was nice of you. Where's the open bar?"

I pointed toward the bar where Cletus was double fisting drinks into his mouth, and she walked off toward it. "Have you met Earlene?" Lucy asked me. "There's the goats!"

A truck parked near us, and two men dressed as shepherds began to file out barnyard animals from the back of it. Spencer came over and put his arm around my waist. "I'm not going to ask about Stalin," he whispered, nuzzling my neck.

"Do you know anything about the animals?"

"That I can help you with," he said. "Harry explained it. They're for atmosphere, to give the event a pastoral feel, like Marie Antoinette playing shepherdess. That sort of thing. Hey, are you wearing panties?" He felt up my butt through my dress. "Nope. Good girl. Maybe we can go home early. Or I can do you up against a tree. That might be fun."

It sounded fun, but his "yeah, right" answer about marriage niggled at my brain, rubbing me the wrong way.

"Do me up against a tree? Really, Spencer? Not very romantic. Here we are at a romantic rehearsal dinner, and you want to 'do me up against a tree?'"

He shrugged. "You can't blame a guy for trying. Hey, Ruth, how's it hangin'?"

Ruth had arrived, wearing a long skirt and velvet blouse with a long strand of pearls. "You're being eaten, Gladie," she told me.

"What?"

But then I felt a tug at my backside.

"You're being eaten by a goat," Spencer said, nonplussed.

"That's what I said," Ruth grumbled. "What's the matter? You don't listen to old ladies? You an ageist?"

The goat had a mouthful of my dress and was eating it like it was a fruit rollup.

"Help. Goat. Help," I said.

Ruth slapped at the goat hard with her clutch purse, but the goat didn't seem to mind and was making a lot of progress with my dress.

"Helluva time not to wear panties," Spencer noted.

"What the hell kind of stupid wedding has goats?" Ruth demanded loudly, walloping the goat with no effect at all. "Sonofabitch farm animal is going to eat this girl, alive. Lucy, would you get your pets in line? What have your guests ever done to you?"

"Goat. Help. Goat," I said.

Spencer tugged the remains of my dress out of the goat's mouth, but it moved on to Ruth's skirt. She wacked it hard with her clutch purse, and Spencer went to help her, but the goat ran backward, with a mouthful of Ruth's skirt still in its mouth. The skirt tore, revealing Ruth's legs up to mid-thigh.

The goats ran off into the woods, and the shepherds went after them.

"Well isn't that just wonderful," Ruth complained. "Lucy Smythe, I don't have the legs for a miniskirt. I'm in my 80s!"

"They make the party look pastoral, old woman,"

Lucy growled at Ruth. "They're scenic, damn it! Don't you know serene ambiance when you see it!"

"Can you see my buttcheeks?" I asked Spencer. "I'm feeling a cold draft back there."

There was a scream inside the tent, and two women ran out shrieking, as they were chased by a donkey and two pigs hell bent on eating their beaded dresses. Lucy turned toward Harry. "Hand me another pill, will ya, honey?"

It took thirty minutes for the wedding planner, the dinner staff, and the shepherds to round up the farm animals and clean up after them. The damage wasn't too bad. Three dresses, two dress pants legs, and a chair and a half had been eaten. But even though the damage wasn't extensive, the animal kingdom distraction threw the timetable out the window. The preacher tapped his foot impatiently under the canopy and complained that he was going to be late to watch the hockey game on television. So he decided to hurry things along.

He put two fingers in his mouth and whistled loud and shrill. "Come on, everybody!" he called. "Bring your ostrich eggshell Lucy-tails over here and park your keisters. I'm only booked for another fifteen minutes, you know."

The preacher must have really liked his hockey. He kept looking at his watch, and he had a Gulls jersey peeking out from under his black blazer. The guests began to shuffle to their seats.

There was an air of trauma and confusion among the guests, and after the animal attacks, more than half of them guzzled down a crap ton of the Lucy-tails. Unfortunately, I wasn't one of them. In the chaos, I hadn't drunk a sip. Instead, I hovered over Lucy, making sure that she was emotionally okay. For some reason, I felt guilty for the disasters in her life. Somewhere inside me, I believed that if I had been a better friend and maid of honor, her rehearsal dinner would have gone off without a hitch.

And she wouldn't have been bald.

So, I hovered around Lucy, who was higher than a kite, while the staff tried to right the chaos, the other guests got sloshed, and Bridget stood by the Stalin cake, explaining to everyone who passed how Stalin strayed from Marx's vision, but that her unborn son Vladimir wouldn't kill millions of people or send millions of others to Siberia.

After spurning Spencer's continuing offers to get me naked in the forest, especially since I was already almost naked, he talked to Uncle Harry and Harry's cronies, who looked like the cast from a Godfather sequel, the later years. I caught snippets of their conversations about poker, boxing, and Harry's epic honeymoon, which going to start right after the wedding.

But as the preacher continued to whistle at us to start

the rehearsal, Spencer took my hand and walked me up the aisle. "This is nice. I like this," he said, as we walked.

"You do?" I asked, surprised.

"Sure. We're on a date, the booze is free, and you're not stumbling over dead people. It's kind of perfect."

"Oh," I said, looking down at the peach-colored carpet, a little disappointed by Spencer's answer.

"I mean, sure you got eaten by a goat, but so did others, and you didn't get your hair burned off. Normally you're the one getting sucked into vacuum cleaners and stuck in pickle jars."

"Actually, those things have never happened to me."

"You know what I mean," he said, giving my hand a squeeze. "You're normally the center of the tornado, the eye of the hurricane, ground zero of thermonuclear war. But lately you've stayed out of it, like you've been dodging the crap and letting it land right on Lucy. I'm proud of you, Pinky. Very proud."

"You make it sound like I won third prize at the grammar school spelling bee."

"Oh, Pinky, you and I both know that could never happen."

He was right. I was a terrible speller.

Under the canopy, there were six of us. Lucy and Harry stood in the center with Bridget and me on Lucy's side and Spencer and Cletus on Harry's side. Cletus was a last-minute addition and he was in charge of Lucy's ring. Lucy's sister, Earlene, was more or less playing the mother-of-the-bride role in the front row. She was drinking her ostrich egg Lucy-tail through a straw, and every few seconds she stuck her fist in the air and shouted, "That's my baby sister! Finally making it legal!"

I tried to focus on Harry and Lucy. They were gazing at each other, like two people completely in love. It was as if the world had fallen away and all that was left was the two of them. It was very romantic. Suddenly, I liked weddings. Suddenly, I forgot about the chaos of the evening, and I only noticed their love and their desire to pledge themselves to each other forever in front of their friends. A tear popped out of my eye, and I wiped it away with my finger.

"No. No. No. This isn't right," the preacher complained, looking at his watch, again. Harry and Lucy seemed to wake out of their reverie and looked at the preacher, questioningly. "The actual couple doesn't do the rehearsal ceremony. The maid of honor and the best man practice the ceremony, and the couple looks on. Okay?"

He shot me a look, and I looked behind me in hopes

that he was talking about Bridget. But he wasn't. Lucy and Harry moved aside.

"Your face is doing that thing again, Gladie," Bridget said.

"Hey legs, if you keep twitching, your nose is going to fall off," Uncle Harry noted.

"I'm not twitching," I said, but I could feel my face doing the cha-cha. Sometimes it sucked being neurotic.

"Come on, Pinky," Spencer said, taking my hand. "I don't bite." He leaned down, his face almost touching mine, and smirked. "But I can start, if you want. And by the way, your ass looks amazing in that dress."

"Dearly beloved," the preacher started.

"She doesn't deserve you, hottie!" Earlene shouted from her seat. "Whoa, Nelly, he is one hot biscuit of love! Listen, honey, she ain't got one-half of what I got! Come over here, and let me take you for a real ride of love!"

"Shut your trap, Earlene!" Cletus yelled, coming to the rescue. I guessed I had mistaken him for a know-nothing hick, because here he was gallant in my time of need. Spencer, meanwhile, was giving me his smirkiest smirk. I wagged my finger at him to stop him before he said something stupid.

"Nobody tells me to shut up!" Earlene yelled.

"It started with a zoo, and now it's a circus," Ruth grumbled from her seat in the third row. Her knees were slightly separated, giving the world a peek at her girdle.

"You should have stopped after the bottle of fireball. But you had to chug the bottle of Captain Morgan, too," Cletus spat at Earlene.

The preacher sighed and looked at his watch, again. "We are gathered together…" He continued the spiel, just like in the movies, and Spencer took my hands in his and looked deep into my eyes, which made my throat close and my nose run. Then I started to cry. Luckily it was a quiet cry, but I was definitely crying. Tears streamed down my cheeks. Spencer's face was the picture of shock and surprise, and all of his fun and humor was sucked out of him. Ditto his smirk. He cupped my face with his hands and wiped my tears away with his thumbs.

"Pinky, you're breaking my heart," he whispered.

"And here's where the ring comes in," the preacher said, unconcerned with my tears. He probably saw a lot of tears in his line of work. "What's that buzzing sound? What the hell?"

At first I thought the buzzing was coming from me, and it was just one more weird thing that my body was doing against my will. But it wasn't coming from me.

"It's an alien invasion," Meryl cried from the third row next to Ruth.

"Smile, it's the photo drones," Lucy said. "They're taking the official photos."

Spencer smirked. "It's the photo drones, Pinky."

Two drones zipped over the guests' heads. They looked like they came right out of a *War of the Worlds* remake. I expected The Rock or Tom Cruise or whoever was the action star of the day to jump out of the bushes and attack the buzzing, flying machines overhead, but nobody made a move against them. Instead, everyone looked up, staring at the drones, and I figured Lucy was going to have a lot of photos of her guests with their necks outstretched, their mouths open, and a look of *what the hell* on their faces.

The buzzing got louder. The drones seemed to get angry. "They're coming right at us," the preacher said. "Are they supposed to do that?"

"I've got it!" Cletus announced, and pulled out a gun. Spencer tackled me to the ground, shielding me with his body, just as the shots rang out. *Boom! Boom!* And then it was over, and the drones crashed into the canopy, knocking it backward and taking a few hairs off the preacher's head.

"Are you all right?" Spencer asked me.

"Oof," I replied. It was enough to satisfy him. He jumped up and grabbed the gun out of Cletus' hand.

"What was that for?" Cletus asked.

"No shooting at the wedding, Cletus. Bad," Spencer said, removing the bullets and pocketing them and the gun.

"That's my gun," Cletus complained.

"And this is my badge," Spencer said, flashing his badge. "And this is my fist. You got any more questions?"

Cletus took a step back. "Nope."

"The ring! The ring!" the preacher yelled.

"Harry, give me another pill," Lucy said. He handed her another one and she popped it into her mouth. It was probably too soon to take another pill, but probably the shooting sobered her enough so it would be all right.

Spencer and I took our places, again. The preacher was talking fast, now, desperate to get home to his flat screen and his hockey game.

"The ring!" he repeated. Cletus hopped to it, running over to the preacher while maintaining an arm-swinging length away from Spencer. Without saying a word, he unhooked his belt and unzipped his pants.

"Uh," I said.

"What are you doing?" the preacher demanded.

"Getting' the ring. What do you think I'm doin'?"

"He's getting the ring," Spencer repeated, smirking at me.

Cletus stuck his hand in his tighty whities and rooted around in it.

"What are you doing?" the preacher demanded, his voice sounding a lot like he was singing soprano at the Met.

"Almost got it," Cletus answered. "Nope, that was something else. Hold on."

"I can't believe what my eyes are seeing," Ruth grumbled. "And my legs are cold. Somebody crank up the heaters. Do you want a dead woman on your hands, frozen to death at a rehearsal dinner?"

The staff, who hadn't fled with the gunshots, moved around adjusting the portable heaters. Finally, Cletus found the ring in his crotch, holding it up above his head, triumphantly. He handed it to Spencer.

"I'm not touching that," Spencer said, making me fall in love with him all over again.

Lucy grabbed it from him. "We have time to sanitize it before the wedding. And you're no longer in charge of the ring. Are we done?"

We weren't done. There was still the kiss. The best part.

"Wait a minute," Cletus said, continuing to root around in his underpants. "I might have given you the wrong ring."

"What did he say?" Ruth asked.

"He's searching his underpants for more rings," Bridget called back.

"How many rings does he have in his drawers?" Meryl asked. It was a good question.

"Damn, he's hot!" Earlene exclaimed and passed out, slumping on one of Uncle Harry's friends who was sitting next to her.

"I've had enough," the preacher said. "If you don't get your hands out of your pants, I'm going to deck you." That was directed at Cletus, obviously, but we all took a step backward, giving the preacher a clear line to Cletus' jaw. The preacher was a big guy, and he looked like he was in shape.

We would never find out if Cletus found more rings in his briefs or if the preacher could knock him out with one punch, because just then a big wind hit us, ruffling all of the women's dresses-- that hadn't been eaten by barnyard animals-- and ripping the tent out of the ground and up into the air.

"I'm thinking that's not supposed to happen," I said to Spencer, watching the tent flying through the air.

"I think we're beyond rules at this point," he said.

The tent flew for a few feet before it was stopped by one of the portable heaters and, in a breathtaking moment, went up into flames and turned into a fireball, rolling along with the heater until it hit the lake where it was finally doused.

"I'm thinking *that's* not supposed to happen," I said.

"Harry, darlin', give me another pill," Lucy said.

"We're out."

Her eyes seemed to bulge out of their sockets, and her face turned red and splotchy. "What do you mean we're out? There's a Stalin cake. My photo drones were shot out of the sky. My ring smells of Cletus's testicles, and the tent blew away."

"You forgot about my dress," Ruth said.

Lucy looked like she was going to blow. In a moment of incredible bravery, I dove for her and wrapped my protective arms around her. "It's okay," I told her. "It's a rehearsal. Think of it this way: You worked out the bugs for the real wedding."

Lucy hugged me back, as if she was holding on for dear life. "Bugs?"

"Yes. No more bugs."

The rehearsal dinner wasn't horrible after that. The staff arranged the heaters around the tables so we weren't cold, and an eight-piece orchestra appeared out of nowhere and played relaxing classical music. I sat at a table with Spencer, Bridget, Ruth, and two of Uncle Harry's old cronies. We were given a four-course meal that started with prime rib and ended with Stalin cake.

At the end of the meal, Spencer leaned over to me and whispered in my ear, sending shockwaves of desire and need through me. "Nothing gets me hotter than watching you scarf down Stalin cake. You make eating a dictator sexy as hell. Frosting porn. I especially get turned on when you grunt when you get going, eating fast like you're afraid that someone's going to steal the cake from you. It's animalistic, like a pig or a pack of hyenas."

I ignored the pig comment because he was really handsome. "Then, give me yours so you can get really turned on," I said, pointing at his untouched cake with my fork.

I ate his after I finished mine and watched his eyes grow dark, his lips redden, and him shift in his seat as his lower body grew uncomfortable. "Let's get out of here," he croaked.

"We have to stay for the rehearsal dinner photo."

"Haven't we suffered enough?"

I took another bite of his cake. "Why? What do you want to do to me? What do you want to do with my body while I just lie there? Tell me everything. Slowly."

"Jesus, Gladie," Ruth complained. "We can hear you, you know. We're sitting at the same table. Stalin's mustache is backing up on me from your bonking talk."

"What? What are they saying?" One of Harry's friends demanded.

"They're getting their freak on," Ruth explained. "They're like wild animals. No manners at all." She wiped her mouth with the back of her hand and belched.

"What's next on this hit parade?" Harry's other friend asked. "I have to get home to take my Lipitor before the prime rib reaches my left ventricle." He gave Ruth a pointed look. "How about you? You want to come home with me? I got a sixteen-hour DVD boxed set about D-Day. And then we could do other things. I have other pills besides Lipitor." He winked at her.

"I'd rather go home with Cletus while I jab myself in the eye with a paring knife," she said. "I'm done. Where's Lucy? We got to get this show on the road."

"Hello, hottie," Earlene said sneaking up behind Spencer. She was holding another ostrich egg Lucy-tail, and she was emitting clouds of alcohol from her pores. "We're about to take the group photo, and I'm going to let you stand next to me." She ran fingers through his hair, messing it up and then put her arm around his chest, slipping her hand under his blazer.

I would have been jealous if I didn't have more cake to eat and if she wasn't drooling on Spencer's perfect hair. With the skill of an experienced hottie who had been hit on by eighty percent of women in Southern California and of a cop who had worked the drunk tank for six months in Los Angeles, he managed to extricate himself from Earlene and wipe his hair with a peach linen napkin.

Just in time, Harry announced that we were ready to take the group photo, which was going to be taken on the dock, backlit with the reflection of the full moon on the lake. Spencer took his blazer off and draped it over my shoulders to shield my ass against the night cold. He put his arm around me.

"Have I mentioned that you look fine tonight?" he asked me.

"You mean fine like just okay or like *fine?*"

"I mean you look as good as Earlene thinks she looks."

That was pretty good. "Smooth talker," I said.

A professional photographer yelled at the guests in a thick Russian accent, ordering everyone to file onto the lake's deck. He organized the people into some kind of aesthetic with Lucy and Harry in front.

"We're one 'cheese' away from me driving you home and ravishing you," Spencer told me, holding me close. "I might use the siren to get us there faster."

"Do you hear that?" I asked.

"My heart? It beats for you."

"No, Casanova. I mean a noise. Like a groan."

Spencer smirked. "Groan? Or moan, cause I'm gonna make you… Hey, what was that?"

"Did you hear it, too?"

"Sounds like the deck is complaining," someone said.

"The deck is complaining," I whispered, repeating the

words and letting them sink into my brain. There was something important about those words, but I was having difficulties processing the information. Why was it bad that the deck was complaining? Why? Why?

Oh, shit.

I threw my hand around Spencer's arm in a death grip. "I have a bad feeling about this," I said.

"Okay, everyone," the photographer ordered. "Take one step to the left."

I prayed that everyone would ignore him and stay put, but they followed directions perfectly. In unison, they stepped left, and the deck complained.

"Are you kidding me?" Spencer said.

CHAPTER 5

There are those of us who dream on the inside and those of us who dream on the outside. You have the gift, bubeleh, just like me and my mother and her mother before her. We have our dreams on the inside. They're vivid and real, and they don't leave us alone. Your father dreamed on the outside, through his poetry. He shared those dreams with the world so others could dream, too. Probably it's better to dream on the outside, dolly. But that's not who we are. Our gift is all inside. It's a terrible burden to have so much inside us, and sometimes it seeps out through cracks and fissures. Be careful when this happens. It can overwhelm folks, and they might not take kindly to it.

Lesson 111, Matchmaking advice from your
Grandma Zelda

The miracle was that only five of us wound up in the

hospital and nobody drowned. But I didn't find that out until later. The deck seemed to fall apart in slow motion, but too fast for the guests to flee for their lives. Also, the photographer was still framing his shot and told everyone to stand still. Still, there was a lot of screaming. A few people dove into the lake, like a scene out of *Titanic,* but Spencer and I were in the center of the melee, and so it was like a bad Who concert for us or a giant people of the masses burrito, heavy on the elbows and knees.

It was all a blur. I don't remember a lot of it after the first batch of clawing fingernails hit me, or maybe that was a chunk of the deck. But I passed out pretty quickly.

"Gladys Burger! Gladys Burger! Wake up, Gladys!"

Don't call me, Gladys, I said, but my lips didn't move and no sound came out. I was probably in a coma, which would be great for losing weight, but probably not great health-wise. On the other hand, I was in a deep sleep. So deep that I didn't care that I needed to pee real badly. That's a really deep sleep. That kind of deep sleep was probably good for preventing wrinkles, too. Maybe I would be in a coma for years and come out in my forties but look like I was nineteen. That would be great. It would be like a painless Botox treatment. So, I loved comas. Comas were awesome. I never wanted to wake up from my coma. I was going to be young forever and never have to pee.

"Wake up, Gladys!"

How annoying. Someone was trying to wake me up so I would get wrinkles and have to pee.

"Gladys!"

My eyes fluttered open, slowly. A bright light was overhead, and a woman was leaning over me, studying me like she was going to wax my mustache, which would have been great because it had been a while and I had more than one mutant hair that needed plucking.

"There you are, Gladys. We thought we lost you there."

"I'm not lost. I know exactly where I am. Where am I?" The smell of antiseptic hit my nostrils and the sounds of machines beeping, nurses complaining, and patients screaming hit my ears. "Am I dying? Am I dying?"

"You're at West Side Hospital. You have a concussion."

"West Side Hospital? A concussion? That must cost forty-thousand dollars here. I don't have any money. I got my health insurance at the bottom of a Captain Crunch box. I won't even tell you where I get my annual PAP smear. Get me out of here. I can literally hear the bill adding up. Did you hear that? *Ka-ching*? I heard it."

"Lucy Smythe is paying your bill," the nurse said.

"She is?" I relaxed. "Oh, okay. I might need a massage, too. That's covered, right?"

I was fine but needed to stay at the hospital for twenty-four hours for observation. I was told that Spencer was somewhere getting a cast, Cletus and Earlene had scrapes and bruises and alcohol poisoning, and Lucy was heavily sedated for emotional stress.

Poor Lucy.

Meanwhile, I was wheeled into the Adele room, which I later found out was on a par with the Sinatra room, but way below the Rihanna and Beyoncé rooms, where Lucy was holed up. The orderly wheeled me inside, past a bed by the door, and parked my bed next to the window. He pulled the curtain around me.

"This is the remote for the entertainment center and here is the call button," the orderly told me and left the room. I pushed a button, and the room was inundated with the scents of sandalwood and lavender.

"What the hell?" I asked out loud.

"You must have pressed the aromatherapy button," a voice told me.

"What?"

My curtain was pulled aside, and a little, old lady peeked her head inside. "Aromatherapy," she said, smiling.

She was about four-feet-ten with long gray hair wrapped up in a bun on the top of her head. Little round glasses were perched on her button nose, and she was round. Her pudgy face had pushed out most of her wrinkles, and so even though she was old, she was very pretty. She was wearing the same pink hospital gown that I was, and her arm was connected to an IV.

"I'm Mrs. Friendly, your roommate," she said. "Gallstones. What are you in for?"

"I think a deck fell on my head, or maybe it was just a wedding party."

Mrs. Friendly shook her head. "Weddings can be rough. I was at one in Palm Springs last month that took down everyone who ate the whitefish salad."

My stomach growled. Whitefish salad sounded good.

"I was about to go hunting for something to eat. They've got me on the gallbladder diet, but I heard that Bobby Flay was here and there's leftovers. You up for it?"

I didn't know what the rule was about eating with a concussion, but I was hungry, and I had never eaten food made by a famous chef. "Sure," I said, swinging my legs off the bed. I was hit with a wave of dizziness, but my head cleared quickly.

"Are you from Cannes?" Mrs. Friendly asked me, as we walked out of the room, wheeling the IV poles with us.

"Yes, I live in the Historic District with my grandmother. And you?"

"I'm just outside. I heard that West Side Hospital was the best so I came here."

"It sure is fancy," I said. It looked like a five-star resort, not a hospital. The floors in the hallways were carpeted, and there was beautiful artwork on the walls. Classical music was piped in at a low level, and there were fountains in every nook and cranny. The nurses were dressed in white resort outfits and ready with smiles and offers of assistance.

We walked down the hallway to where Mrs. Friendly suspected the leftovers were kept. We passed several rooms, and I peeked in. There were different levels of luxury with some rooms featuring canopy beds.

As we passed one room, there was loud groaning. "Holy halls of Dixie," a man groaned. I knew that voice. It was hard to forget the man who had stuffed the wedding ring in his underpants. I popped my head into the room.

"Hello, Cletus. How are you doing?"

He was sitting on his bed, throwing up into a bucket. Earlene was roomed with him. She had been sleeping in the bed by the door, but she opened her eyes when I spoke.

"I thought you were dead," she said to me.

"Concussion," I said.

"That's good. I wish I were dead."

"Now, now," Mrs. Friendly said. "They're going to take good care of you. Chin up."

"Who are you?"

"This is Mrs. Friendly," I said.

"Gallstones," Mrs. Friendly explained. "We're off to search for barbecue leftovers. Should we bring you back some?"

"I could go for some barbecue," Cletus said and threw up again in his bucket.

I took that as our signal to leave. Mrs. Friendly was right about the leftovers. We found them on a beautifully wood carved table in a designer dining room. "Yum," Mrs. Friendly said. We found china plates and crystal goblets in a side board and some containers with various salads in a small refrigerator, which was disguised as a cabinet.

We piled our plates high and dug in.

"Gladie Burger," Mrs. Friendly said, looking up at the ceiling. "I used to know a Zelda Burger."

"That's my grandmother."

"We were on a cruise to Alaska together." That had to be years ago because my grandmother had been a shut-in since my father had died. "She won a mint at roulette, if memory serves. It was like she had a sixth sense about where the numbers were going to land."

"Well, well, well, what do we have here?" the orderly asked, walking into the room. "I'm not sure that ribs are good for gallstones. But don't worry. I won't tell."

He took a can of soda out of the refrigerator and sat down at the table. "How are we doing, ladies?"

"Dandy," Mrs. Friendly said.

"Okay," I said, but actually I was feeling queasy. The barbecue food was better in theory than it was in my stomach. Mrs. Friendly gave me a knowing look.

"Maybe you should save the rest for later," she suggested, kindly.

"Good idea," I said.

"I'll get a box and put it in the fridge for you," the orderly offered. He handed me a Styrofoam box and I put the food in it. I was feeling worse and worse. Mrs. Friendly took the box from me and finished filling it up. She closed it and took a Sharpie from the orderly and wrote my name on the box. Then, she drew a design under my name.

"That's Greek for 'don't touch,'" she explained. "I used to teach classics."

I was ready to go back to bed and sleep. "Do you know if Spencer Bolton is okay?" I asked the orderly.

"The big guy? The cop? He's been asking about you nonstop. I told him I would take him to visit you once his cast is set. They're body casting him to support the arm."

That sounded bad, and worry bubbled up in me and took over, increasing my nausea. The orderly seemed to read my thoughts. He patted my back. "He's fine. Ornery. You'll see him just as soon as they're done with him. I promise."

I took a deep breath to steady my emotions and my nausea.

Mrs. Friendly handed the box to the orderly and stood. "I think we're done here. Let's get you back in bed, Gladie."

The walk back to our room took longer and was harder than the walk from our room. Exhaustion washed over me, but at least the nausea had died down to a bearable level. In the hallway, a patient walked toward us, but he was in obvious pain. His legs were wide apart, like he had something hidden under his gown.

"Good evening," Mrs. Friendly said, brightly.

The man put his head down. "Good evening." He shuffled past us a little faster but still in obvious pain. West Side looked like a resort, but it didn't change the fact that it was a hospital and filled with people who were sick and suffering.

When we got back to our room, we both slipped into our beds, and the moment that my head hit the pillow, I fell into a deep sleep.

I woke up a couple hours later when the nurse wrapped a blood pressure cuff around my arm. "Hello, sleepy head," she said. She looked different than she did when I had first seen her. She was blue. In fact, the whole room was blue.

"The room looks weird," I said.

"That's the healing light," she said, quietly. Besides the blue light, the room was dark, and the hospital had turned silent. "How are you feeling?"

"Fine." The nausea had gone, but I was still exhausted. "I've forgotten your name."

"Milly," she said and stuck a thermometer under my tongue. After taking my vitals, Milly offered me a pore-closing face mask and a hand massage. I accepted both of them. "How about music? There's some good smooth jazz I could pipe into the room, and then the mood lighting will change with the beat. Very healing. Very relaxing."

"No, thank you. I don't want to wake up Mrs. Friendly."

"Who?"

"Mrs. Friendly. My roommate."

Milly fluffed my pillow. "What do you mean?"

"The woman in the next bed." I looked to my left, but there was no one there. No bed, either.

"This is a single room, miss. Just you."

"But Mrs. Friendly was here. Remember when you wheeled me in here? You moved me by the window."

But now I was in the center of the room, and the nurse was right. I was alone. There was no sign of Mrs. Friendly.

"Is she okay?" I asked the nurse. "She seemed fine, but she had gallstones. Are gallstones bad?"

"I don't know Mrs. Friendly," Milly said, calmly, like

I was wielding a knife, and she had to convince me not to stab her in the eye. She dragged a chair by the bed and sat down, taking my hand in hers, and she started to massage it. "You know, sometimes concussions can cause some issues."

The hair on my arms stood up. "Issues? What kind of issues?"

"Like memories of things that didn't happen. You were out cold. You probably dreamed about your mysterious Mrs. Friendly."

Did I dream an entire conversation with a woman? Did I have brain damage? Was I having hallucinations without getting high first? I had no doubt I could have wishfully thought my way to a barbecue meal, but Mrs. Friendly was so real. No way had I made her up. I might have had a concussion, but I was still in my right mind.

I took my hand back from Milly's talented, massaging fingers. "No, I didn't dream her up. She was here for gallstones. I can even tell you what she looked like."

"Please stay calm, Miss Burger. We don't want you to take a turn for the worse."

I sat up in bed. "Listen, she existed. Exists, I mean. Instead of patronizing me, can you just check the records? Her last name is Friendly. I don't know her first name, but I doubt you have more Friendlys here."

Milly kept her I'm-talking-to-a-crazy-person face on while she backed out of the room.

While she was gone, I replayed my time in the hospital over and over in my head. Yes, I had been unconscious when I had been brought to the hospital, but after that, I had been completely lucid. I couldn't have made up Mrs. Friendly. I had spoken with her, eaten with her.

The nurse returned with a tall man, who had a goatee and was wearing a white doctor's coat. He smiled kindly at me and took a seat on my bed next to me. He had nice breath, like minty mouthwash. He was youngish, about forty years old. I liked him immediately.

"I'm Doctor Fric," he said in a soft voice. "I'm so sorry this is happening to you."

"To me? No, it's happening to Mrs. Friendly. There was a woman here, you see, but she's vanished. I'm worried about her."

Dr. Fric nodded, and his face grew serious, as if he was worried about Mrs. Friendly too and was going to get right on it for me. But I read him wrong. He wasn't worried about the disappeared old lady. He was worried about me.

"What you've experienced isn't out of the ordinary for brain trauma," he explained.

"Brain trauma? I have brain trauma?" I didn't want

brain trauma. Just thinking about having brain trauma was giving me trauma. I touched my head. Yep, I was traumatized.

"We're going to make sure you're completely fine. I promise that we will take good care of you."

"But what about Mrs. Friendly?"

Dr. Fric's eyebrows knitted together, as if it hurt him to give me this news. "We've scoured our records, Miss Burger, and we've searched our little hospital, and we've never had a Mrs. Friendly here, and there is currently nobody here being treated for gallstones."

The news hit me like a wrecking ball to my head, and I touched my temples in pain. If there had been no Mrs. Friendly, I had more than brain trauma. I was losing my mind.

CHAPTER 6

I've been a widow for a lot of years, dolly. So, I know about being alone, about not having a partner in life. People come to us, and they want different things. Some want regular sex without a condom. Some want a diamond ring. Some want a dinner companion. Some want children. That's all easy to get for them. We could pick any Tom, Dick, or Jane off the street, and it would be a job well done. But even if they don't know it, the real reason we're here is to get them what they really want. What they really need. I don't mean a fakakta ring. I mean a partner. Someone for them to go through the ups and downs with. Someone to share the good mazel and the bad mazel. Someone who's got their back. If they got that, they got everything.

Lesson 16, Matchmaking advice from your
Grandma Zelda

"I'm not crazy," I said into Dr. Fric's deep brown eyes and thoughtful expression.

"Of course you're not crazy," he said. "But I do think I should re-examine you, just so we're sure we didn't miss anything."

My ears perked up and my skin sprouted goosebumps. "You missed something? Like what? Like… cancer?" I said *cancer* in a whisper, in case saying it out loud would give me the evil eye.

Dr. Fric put his hand on my arm to calm me. "I'm sure we didn't miss a thing, but I have to do my job. You don't want me to fall down on the job, now would you?" He gave a dose of his winning smile and winked at me. "What kind of doctor would I be if I did that? They would take away my diploma. Boy would my mother be upset if they did that."

He shined a light in my eyes.

"But what do you mean miss something?" I asked. "I mean, what are you looking for? Like… brain tumors? I use a cellphone, you know. I put it right up against my head. I know I shouldn't do that, but I do each time. Dr. Fric, I don't want a brain tumor. Please don't let me have a brain tumor."

"It would be very rare to find a brain tumor."

"Rare? Rare? So we're talking it's possible? I don't want a brain tumor. You would have to cut it out of my head. I'm not a doctor, but I'm reasonably sure that it would hurt to cut into my brain."

Dr. Fric kept smiling and slipped his little flashlight into his jacket pocket. "Actually, fun fact: there's no pain receptors in the brain."

"Fun fact? Fun facts are that the Cannes Speedy Mart sells week-old muffins for half-off. Another fun fact is that my heel calluses can be used to scrub out the bathtub ring. There are no fun facts that have to do with brain surgery. No fun. No fun." I clutched his jacket. "Please don't cut open my head."

Gently, he removed my hands from his jacket and continued to examine me. "No one's going to cut open your head. Probably not, I mean," he said.

I tried to relax while he continued to examine me, but really I was just trying not to throw up from the anxiety. My heart must have been going a mile a minute. I was fine, I told myself. My head felt fine. My eyesight was clear. I wasn't seeing people who weren't there...at least I was reasonably sure that everyone I was seeing was actually there. How would I know if they weren't? Oh, brain trauma was a sick bitch. I needed Spencer. He would never let me see people who weren't there and he wouldn't let anyone cut open my head.

He would make a crack about how there was nothing in my head so why would anyone want to open it.

So, I was fine. I was totally and completely fine.

"Ow!" I shouted. A pain shot up from my abdomen where the doctor was pushing on it. It was a terrible pain. Dr. Fric shook his head, like he was disappointed.

"Okay," he said, standing. "Your head is fine."

"It is?"

"Yes. But I'm afraid your appendix is not so fine."

"My what?"

"I have an opening tomorrow morning at ten. We'll take it out, then. Don't worry. I've done a million of these. No big deal."

"But…"

"Nurse, start the paperwork on that." Nurse Millie nodded like it was no big and they were discussing ordering dim sum from the local Chinese takeout.

"But…" I said.

The doctor patted my shoulder and walked toward a door. "See you in the morning," he said, waving his hand above his head as he left.

"But…"

The nurse fluffed my pillow. "You're in good hands. He's a great surgeon. No food until after the surgery, okay? Do you need anything else?"

I had no words. I wanted to escape, run away. I had never had an operation before. I still had my wisdom teeth and my tonsils. I had a terrible fear of doctors and hospitals and now I was in the middle of it. Surgery. I was going to have surgery. A few hours before, I was flirting with Spencer, ready to go home and let him do all kinds of fun things to me, and now I was waiting to have an operation. I wanted to run away. I wanted to get out of there on the double. How could I escape? Oh, why did my body turn on me? Why couldn't my appendix work like it was supposed to?

Come to think of it, what did an appendix do, anyway?

"I don't think so?" I said like a question because I didn't think she would help me break out.

As she left the room, the orderly came in, pushing a mop. I bolted from my bed. With the talk about my impending surgery, I had forgotten about Mrs. Friendly. Poor Mrs. Friendly had disappeared, and nobody knew where she was or even that she had existed. But the orderly had met her and spoken with the both of us. He was my proof that I wasn't crazy and that I didn't hallucinate or dream about the missing old lady. He might know where she was, too.

"There you are!" I shouted. "You're my witness!"

He froze in place. "Excuse me?"

"Poor Mrs. Friendly has disappeared and nobody knows where she is," I explained, relieved that finally I had someone who could vouch for me.

The orderly squinted and gripped his mop. "I'm sorry. Who's that?"

"The old lady I was with just a few hours ago. Remember? We were eating barbecue, and you gave her a box to put the leftovers in?"

He shook his head. "I remember you from when they brought you in. I brought you a heated blanket, remember?"

I didn't remember the heated blanket at all and I remembered nothing from when they brought me into the hospital. I didn't want to tell him that though, because I didn't think that would help my cause.

"We talked about Spencer Bolton. You told me that he was worried about me and that he was getting a cast put on," I reminded him.

His face brightened and he smiled. "Oh, yeah. I remember that."

"Finally!" I exclaimed.

"We talked about that when you came in. You were very worried."

"No. But. No," I stammered. "We were eating barbecue. Remember? And we talked about Mrs. Friendly's gallstones?"

He shrugged. "Gallstones? Barbecue? I'm sorry. That doesn't ring a bell and I don't remember ever meeting a Mrs. Friendly."

I shut my eyes. This was a nightmare. I was going to have my appendix removed, and I was going crazy. Just as I finally had a career and a relationship, I was going to lose it all. My brain had created a person who never existed and conversations that never happened. I realized that I even had the taste of barbecue in my mouth.

"I'm that far gone," I moaned.

"Are you all right? Do you want me to call the nurse?" the orderly asked.

"No, that's okay," I moaned.

The orderly continued to mop my floor, careful to keep his head down and not make eye contact with the crazy woman. The second he finished, I decided to find Spencer. I needed support. I had created a person that didn't exist, and I had an impending operation. I couldn't handle freaking out alone.

I found Spencer on the floor above me. At first I didn't recognize him and walked right by his room. As I passed his room, I thought, "poor bastard," but then I heard his voice, as he growled on the phone. He was lying in bed with his left arm outstretched at an angle in a cast, supported by a metal rod connected to his chest, which was also wrapped in a cast.

"Detective, this is not a promotion. I'm only out for a couple of days," he said into the phone. I couldn't imagine him going back to work like he was, but Spencer took his job as chief of police very seriously. "I don't care what you've heard, Remington. I'm fine. Don't screw up my squad while I'm out!"

He slammed the phone down on the table over his bed and he noticed me. His face altered from the frustrated police chief to the in-love boyfriend. "Hey there, Pinkie," he said, softly. "I was worried about you, but you look damned good. No worse for wear. Not like me. I guess this means you're going to be on top for a few weeks."

Tears filled my eyes and dropped down my face.

"What's the matter, Pinky?"

I ran to Spencer and put my head on his chest, ignoring his *oomph* as I made impact. "I have to have an operation," I said.

"Please God, tell me it's not a breast reduction."

I slapped his belly, and he *oomphed,* again. "Appendix. They're going to take my appendix out tomorrow."

Spencer combed my hair with his fingers. "I had that operation. No sweat. You'll be fine, and I'll be here to take care of you."

I lifted my head and wiped my nose with the back of my hand. "Really?"

"Of course. It turns out that I have some time in my schedule, and besides, I dig lime Jell-O."

I sniffed. "I'm not allowed to eat until after the surgery."

"That's rough, Pinky." He wiped my cheeks with the fingers of his right hand. "Lean down and let me kiss you."

I leaned down and lightly touched his lips. His right hand touched the back of my head and pulled me closer, capturing my mouth with his and using his tongue to make my head spin. This time, it wasn't the concussion making me dizzy, and I didn't care if it lasted forever.

It didn't last forever, but it did go on for a while, until I got weak in the knees and struggled to stand. "You do that well," I breathed.

"Only my arm is broken, Pinky. The rest of me is raring to go. How's your appendix?"

"Doesn't hurt a bit." It didn't. With all my stress about Mrs. Friendly, I had forgotten to be in pain.

"If the nurse didn't pop in here every couple minutes, I would suggest that we test the strength of this bed," Spencer said, moving his eyebrows up and down, as if he was Groucho Marx. There was some impressive tenting going on with his hospital gown, which led me to believe he wasn't lying about being raring to go. But I couldn't think about sex while I was losing my mind and about to be cut open.

"That's okay. I probably shouldn't jostle my appendix."

"I have to admit that I'm relieved," he said. "When I saw your face, I thought you stumbled on another dead body, but you've really kept your nose clean lately, Pinky."

I slapped my forehead. "I almost forgot!"

"Uh oh."

I sat in the chair next to his bed and told him all about Mrs. Friendly and how I might have brain trauma. He arched an eyebrow when I mentioned my brain, but otherwise, he seemed calm and resigned to my story.

"What do you think?" I asked after I finished.

"I think that you can't keep out of trouble."

"What trouble? It's not my fault that I have a concussion."

"Not that. The woman. Mrs. Friendly."

I was shocked. "You believe me?" I asked, sucking in air. It was the last thing I expected. Normally, Spencer was the first to tell me to stay out of things, and I figured he would have jumped at the idea that I was seeing things and had lost my mind.

"Help me up into the wheelchair," Spencer said, struggling to get up. I gave him my arm and tugged him into a sitting position.

"What are you doing?"

"Going with you to search for Mrs. Friendly. Listen, Pinky, since I met you, you've been stumbling on murders left and right. If you say that a woman has vanished, I have to take you seriously, no matter how much I'd rather get a shot of morphine and sleep for the next twelve hours."

The idea that Spencer would rather search for Mrs. Friendly with me than get a shot of morphine made me feel giddy all over, like we had taken a huge leap forward in our relationship. I helped him into a wheelchair. I had to take off one of the side rails to make room for his left arm, which was sticking out to the side in the cast.

"Not that I don't think this will all be cleared up, Pinky. But so far, all you've got is a concussion and appendicitis. I need to be there to make sure nothing else happens. Who knows what else could befall you while you're snooping."

"You're the one in the body cast," I pointed out.

"And you don't remember why that is?"

I had a vague memory of the deck collapsing. "You tried to help me," I said, remembering.

Spencer nodded. "And then…"

"I grabbed onto a piece of the deck."

He smirked. "And…"

"Okay. Okay. I might have panicked."

Spencer arched an eyebrow. "And you wacked the hell out of me, as I tried to save you. You missed your calling, Pinky. You should have played in the Majors. You have quite a swing."

I felt guilty about injuring Spencer. "I'm sorry. I didn't mean to…"

He grabbed a handful of my butt and gave it a squeeze. "I know you didn't mean to, Pinky. Kind of goes with the territory. I knew the danger before I ever got in your pants." He pulled me down and gave me an I'm-Tarzan-You're-Jane kiss, which either made my concussion worse or cured me, completely.

Spencer showed me how to disconnect our IVs so that we would be freer to search the hospital with me pushing his wheelchair. "We're doing this my way," he said before we left his room.

"What way is that?"

"Nothing crazy. Don't play with dead bodies. Don't let any dogs shoot anybody. Don't go after fake owls. No cults. No body parts in the trash."

I put my hands on my hips. "I've never played with a dead body."

"You wheeled one around Ruth's sisters' house."

"Oh, yeah, that's right."

"So, basically, if you think of it, stop yourself and

don't do it. I'm in charge," he said. I pursed my lips. "Damn it, Pinky. I'm a professional. I know what I'm doing. And if we don't find Mrs. Friendly, we'll chalk it up to a weird drug reaction. Deal?"

I gnawed on the inside of my cheek. Spencer and I both knew that I would never let him be in charge, and he also knew that things just happened to me without any effort of my own. "None of those things were my fault," I insisted. "The owl, the cult, I was just an innocent bystander."

"Deal?" he repeated, putting his hand out.

I shook it. "Deal."

But my other hand was behind my back with my fingers crossed.

CHAPTER 7

Search and ye shall find. I think that was Shakespeare or maybe the Bible. Or it could have been Morty Lieberman, my father's accountant. He was a very wise man. Anyway, yes, sometimes if you search, you will find. Remember that time I lost my favorite hat? I searched and searched and finally found it under my mattress. Sure, the hat wasn't my favorite after it had been smooshed under me for a week, but I found it! But there's a lot we don't find, even if we search like a bloodhound. Usually, we don't find what we're looking for because we don't understand what we're looking for. For instance, Kevin Simon wanted a woman who was size two with brown eyes and red hair and could yodel. Kevin Simon was a shmuck. He never found that woman, and when I presented him with Cynthia Levin, who won first prize in the Atlantic City yodeling contest but had green eyes, red hair, and was a size twelve, well Kevin Simon wouldn't even talk to her. "Why don't you find what I'm looking for, Zelda?" he asked me. "Because you're a shmuck and don't know what you're looking for," I answered. It's a good thing to be sure about what you're looking for before you start looking in the sofa cushions...

Lesson 72, Matchmaking advice from your
Grandma Zelda

The hospital was four stories tall. My room was on the second story, and Spencer's the third, with the emergency room on the first floor. The lobby looked more like a modern art museum than the entrance to a hospital. There was a lot of money there, and without Lucy and Harry's hand-out, I would never have seen West Side Hospital. It was how the other half lived, and I was grateful that if I had to get my appendix out, at least it was in a fancy shmancy place where I was getting the finest care.

It was now eleven o'clock, and the nurses were changing shifts quietly because most of the patients were sleeping. Spencer and I got some weird looks as the couple in matching hospital gowns, me pushing his chair up and down the hallways. But nobody bothered us while we peeked into every open door. It wasn't the most thorough of searches considering most of the doors were closed up for the night, but we looked into enough rooms to feel defeated.

There was no sign of Mrs. Friendly.

It was looking more and more like I had lost my mind.

"You haven't lost your mind," Spencer said, reading my thoughts. "You were just trippin' off some good pharmaceuticals."

I didn't tell him that I had only been given saline in my IV, and I didn't think saltwater could make me hallucinate. "I'll take you back to your room," I said, crestfallen.

Just as I lost all hope, the man who had been walking down the hall with his legs wide apart while I was with Mrs. Friendly came walking toward us in the hallway. He looked exactly like he had before, pushing his IV bar, walking toward Spencer and me with his legs wide apart and still in obvious pain.

A witness. My hope returned to find Mrs. Friendly.

"Oh my God. Oh my God," I said. "Him! Him!"

I rocked back on my heels and pushed the wheelchair forward, running down the hallway toward the mystery man with his legs wide apart, as if he had elephant balls or some kind of problem with his crotch.

"You!" I said, reaching him. He averted his gaze and lowered his head, like he was a movie star and I was a mob of paparazzi. Maybe he was shy, I thought, or maybe he really was a movie star. I studied his face, but he wasn't any movie star I recognized.

"Remember me?" I asked.

"Yes, sure. Hello. My doctor wants me to walk. Good night."

He tried to shuffle around me, but I pushed Spencer's wheelchair in front of him, blocking his path. Skidding to a halt, Spencer almost fell out of the chair but managed to right himself with his one good hand.

"Tell him about the old lady I was with," I urged the man.

"What?"

"The old lady. Mrs. Friendly. She's vanished. Disappeared. Come on, let's go to security. Maybe the police…" I shot a look at Spencer, and he flinched. "Or the FBI. We probably need to call the feds, in case she was kidnapped."

"Feds? Police?" the man asked and shook his head violently, waving his hand, as if he could wave me away.

"But Mrs. Friendly," I urged him. "There's a woman who needs our help. This is a big deal. You would be in the news for helping."

"Sir," Spencer interrupted. "Do you remember the old woman who was with my friend? The one who disappeared?"

"No. I don't know what she's talking about. I'm just doing my walking, like the doctor told me to do. But now I'm tired and I want to get back to my room."

"Don't you remember?" I asked. "We said hello. She was an old lady with little round glasses. You have to remember her."

"I remember you, walking around here with him," he said, pointing at Spencer. "But no old lady. Please let me go."

"No. You saw us. You saw us."

"No, I didn't. Let me go."

I was holding on to his arm for dear life, like he was my last chance for sanity.

"Let him go," Spencer told me. He tried to move the chair, but he couldn't bend his body because of the body cast. Then, he tried to stand, but he couldn't do that by himself, either. "Damn it to hell. Gladie, let the man go."

"But…"

Reluctantly, I let him go, and he shuffled off without looking back. "She was so real," I told Spencer. "I could smell her perfume. She had a dimple on her right cheek. Her boobs were really saggy."

"All good details, Pinky, especially the boobs part. That's an image that will stay in my head for a long time. I hate to tell you this, but it's looking more and more like you had some kind of LSD flashback. Or a delayed shrooms episode. Saggy boobs and all. It's okay that this time your Miss Marple instincts went haywire. Even Sherlock Holmes had his down days, you know. I'm sure that Jessica Fletcher screwed the pooch on occasion."

"How dare you. Jessica Fletcher never screwed the pooch."

"I'm sure there was a moment in the sixties where she might have screwed the pooch," Spencer said, as if he personally knew Jessica Fletcher.

I sighed. I was losing confidence in myself, but I couldn't let it go. Mrs. Friendly's disappearance didn't make sense and I refused to believe that I had hallucinated the whole thing.

"I swear that Mrs. Friendly was so real. If only I could find someone who remembers her. Wait a second. Cletus and Earlene! They met her. We have to find Cletus and Earlene."

"We've already searched the hospital and I'm pretty sure that the supporting rod in my cast is boring a hold through my ribcage," Spencer said. "Maybe we can re-start this tomorrow morning? We can go back to my room and I'll let you play with Mr. Winky."

Out of the corner of my eye, I saw Nurse Millie walking toward us.

"That's an awesome offer, but we have to find Cletus and Earlene. They'll prove that I was right. They met Mrs. Friendly."

"Mr. Winky wants you to be his Mrs. Friendly."

"You're five years old."

Spencer put his right hand up in a half-shrug. "A guy's gotta keep trying, even if he's wrapped in plaster. Hey, speaking of plaster, I think I've figured out how we can make this whole thing work in bed. I mean, for me."

"This won't take long," I said, ignoring his Mr. Winky talk. "Cletus and Earlene's room is on this floor. In five minutes, this can all blow over and we can finally find poor Mrs. Friendly."

Spencer sighed. "So what are we talking about? Bad news for Mr. Winky?"

"Why do I have the feeling that we have different priorities?"

"Hello, what are we doing up?" Millie, the nurse, asked, reaching us. Her best nurse's smile was planted on her face.

"Uh…" I said.

"I was worried that you would be up. We must get you back to bed and rested for your surgery."

I was angry at Millie for not remembering Mrs. Friendly. "What about you, Millie? Isn't your shift over?"

"I'm doing a double shift," she said. "Time to go to bed, Miss Burger. You're not still looking for the woman you hallucinated?"

"No," I said. My lower lip quivered. Tears threatened to pop out of my eyes. I hated that nobody believed me.

"We were looking for a place to get it on," Spencer said.

Millie blinked twice. "Excuse me?"

"I have a bucket list of strange places to hook up, so we were hoping to get access to the dialysis room. That's number forty-three on my list. I heard they have kickass recliners in there."

I mouthed *thank you* to him. Even though he was a royal pain in the ass and had a permanent frat boy attitude, it was nice to know that he would always have my back.

"You-you-you can't do that," Millie insisted, although I did notice a flush in her cheeks and her eyes flicked toward Spencer's crotch. I couldn't blame her. Thoughts of hooking up with him in the dialysis room had me warm, too.

"Millie, I promise to go back to my room right after I talk to Cletus and Earlene. They met Mrs. Friendly and they can prove that she existed."

Millie sighed and rolled her eyes. "Fine," she said after a moment, surprising me. "Let me just check on them. If they're not sleeping and they agree to be questioned, I'll let you in. Do we have a deal?"

I nodded, hopping on my heels, overjoyed that I was a step closer to proving myself.

Millie turned around and walked down the hallway.

"See?" I said to Spencer. "Miss Marple is back. Miss Marple has got it all goin' on."

"Hey, I'm a big fan of Miss Marple. Miss Marple isn't wearing a bra under her hospital gown. What's not to like?"

"We'll have to pull out all the stops. I'll be in charge of the investigation, of course."

Spencer arched an eyebrow. "That'll be the day. Leave

any investigation to the professionals, Pinky. You're not a professional."

"Ouch. That hurt, Spencer. I need a trigger warning before you say something like that."

"What's a trigger warning?"

"I don't know. I read it in the New Yorker."

He leaned forward and pursed his lips. "*You* read the New Yorker?"

"Fine. I heard it on Desperate Housewives."

Millie came back. Her serious nurse face had returned. "Okay. Two minutes and no more. I need to get in control of my floor. I can't have patients wandering around, upsetting each other."

"Boy, she sure has you pegged," Spencer whispered to me.

I pushed Spencer's wheelchair and followed the nurse to Cletus and Earlene's room. She opened the door. Not only were Cletus and Earlene not asleep, but Earlene was binge-watching Netflix, while Cletus played videogames. He stopped when he saw us.

"How's your hangovers?" I asked.

"All better now," Earlene said. "I could go for a

Bloody Mary, but they refused to give me one."

"I told you that I can get you a milkshake," Millie offered.

"Don't worry, Sis," Cletus said. "I got a flask in my pants. Wow, man, what happened to you?"

"A couple broken bones," Spencer answered.

"Man, you look bad. All good in the you-know-where area?" Cletus asked, touching his own crotch. "Probably should have taped down your junk. It would have protected you."

"Uh…" Spencer said.

"Cletus, Earlene, do you remember the lady I was with before?" I asked, interrupting the junk talk.

"Before what?" Earlene asked.

"We walked by. I was with Mrs. Friendly and she had gallstones."

Cletus and Earlene's foreheads turned into thick lines, as if they were trying to understand my words.

"Mrs. Friendly," I repeated. "Gallstones. She was an old lady, and she was with me. We said we were going to get barbecue, you said you wanted some. Don't you remember?"

Earlene looked up at the ceiling tiles and Cletus resumed his videogame. There was a loud crack of thunder and the entire hospital shook. The lights flickered and went off. It was a sign of my doom, a sign that Cletus and Earlene had no memory of Mrs. Friendly.

"The backup generator will kick into gear, and the lights will come back on," the nurse said, and sure enough, they did. There was another crack of thunder and the hospital shook again. It was like we were under attack. Through the window, we could see flashes of lightning and the wind whipping up the trees.

"You need to go back to your room. I better go check on my patients," the nurse said and left.

I took a couple of steps into the room and wagged my finger at Earlene. "Stop messing around," I growled. "You're coming with me and you're going to tell everyone about Mrs. Friendly. She's missing and she needs us."

At least I thought she did. Nobody disappeared like that without needing help.

"Lucy's friend, we don't know what you're talking about. You're a babe, but you're kind of a pain in the ass," Cletus said.

"Thank you," Spencer said. "If I had a nickel for every time I've said that."

"Does she have a problem?" Earlene asked, moving her finger round and round next to her ear. "Like maybe she got kicked in the head by a mule?"

"That happened to our cousin Bubba years ago," Cletus explained. "Mule got him right in the back of the head. Pow! For the rest of his life, he thought his mother was General Robert E. Lee. On Mother's Day, he gave her a sword and burned down the neighbor's house. The neighbors were Yankees from Maine, who moved to our town to run the Piggly Wiggly. Bubba thought he was gonna get a medal of valor for that one."

"Poor Bubba," Earlene said. "Instead of a medal, he got fifteen to life, which was over in six months, cause he dropped dead in his cell. They called it the ticking time bomb. An artery in his brain had gone bad from the mule kick. One day that artery went *pop!* Poor Bubba was living on borrowed time."

Cletus nodded, sadly, putting his hand on his chest. "Borrowed time. That's probably what you got," he said, pointing at me. "Tick. Tock."

He went back to playing his video game, and I looked at Spencer, whose mouth had dropped open. Without saying another word, I wheeled him out of the room and closed the door behind me. The storm was still going strong outside, but it wasn't anything like what was going on inside me. I was the queen of sympathy pains and psychosomatic illnesses. Instead of Cletus and Earlene making me feel better about my brain, they had ratcheted up my freak out to monumental proportions.

In the hallway, Spencer took my hand and brought it to his lips. "Pinky? You okay?"

"You mean besides the ticking time bomb in my brain?"

"You weren't hit by a mule. You don't have a ticking time bomb. You don't think you're Robert E. Lee."

"Spencer, I made up a woman and I made up eating barbecue. I have a ticking time bomb."

"The doctor examined you and said your brain is fine, and no matter how much I want to crack fifteen jokes about your brain not being fine, I'm sure it really is. Now your appendix is a different matter. You should rest until tomorrow's surgery."

"My appendix does hurt now," I agreed, touching the left side of my belly. "And my stomach is swollen."

"Your appendix is on the other side," Spencer said.

"Mine isn't. It's over here," I said.

"But…"

"I know I should be obsessing about my appendix, but all I can think about is Mrs. Friendly. She was a very nice lady, Spencer, and she disappeared, and now I might be crazy."

As the words left my mouth, they hit me hard and filled me with dread. Appendix, disappeared lady, crazy. None of those things were good. And the worst of it was that I wasn't any closer to finding Mrs. Friendly, which meant that I was getting way closer to being crazy and to getting an organ cut out of my body.

Then a miracle happened. A skinny lady with huge duck lips appeared, like she was a burning bush and I was Moses with a desperate need to be told what to do.

"Are you talking about Mrs. Friendly?" she asked me. She had snuck up behind me in her hot pink velour track suit.

I whipped around and clutched her shoulders. "You know Mrs. Friendly? You've seen her?"

"I love Mrs. Friendly," she said, looking off in the distance.

Jackpot. Finally, someone knew her. I hadn't made her up. I wasn't crazy. "Do you know where she is?"

The skinny woman nodded, vigorously. "Sure. I'm on my way there, now. Why don't you come, too?"

elise sax

CHAPTER 8

Who to trust? It's hard to know. That's why we make the big bucks, dolly. We're the love mavens. We match good people. Good with good. Bad with nobody. But not everyone is a maven. Not everyone has the gift. When matches go out in the world on their own, they worry. They'll ask you: "Should I trust him?" "Should I trust her?" This is what you say: "Trust yourself." Trust you. That might be the hardest person to trust, bubeleh.

Lesson 115, Matchmaking advice from your
Grandma Zelda

"Come with me," the skinny woman with huge duck lips told me. Her entire body was as big around as my leg. She was a walking advertisement for skin and bones. But she was sprightly for someone who had obviously starved herself for the past thirty years. Pushing Spencer in his chair, I had to run to keep up with her. She reached the elevator and pushed the down button.

"Where are we going?" Spencer asked me.

"Where are we going?" I asked the skinny woman.

"The midnight healing circle at integrative medicine downstairs," she said, smiling. Her teeth were bright white and she was wearing diamond earrings that were the size of brass buttons on a man's winter coat. She oozed money.

"Do you work here?" I asked. She probably owned the hospital. She had an air of trust fund around her.

"You'll love the healing circle," she told Spencer. "It does wonders. Everybody benefits from it."

The elevator arrived and I backed Spencer into it, but I misjudged the space and knocked his casted arm into the wall. He winced and I patted his head. "You'll be okay," I said. The skinny lady pushed the button for the ground floor. "So, Mrs. Friendly will be at the healing circle?" I asked her.

"Everyone's welcome," she said.

"So, Mrs. Friendly will be there? You know Mrs. Friendly, right?"

I was getting a bad feeling about the skinny woman, but I pushed it aside in hopes that I was finally going to find

Mrs. Friendly and prove to the world that I hadn't lost my mind.

The elevator doors opened, and the skinny woman walked out. After we left the elevator, Spencer urged me to stop.

"Pinky, I'm feeling strange."

I crouched down in front of him and put my hands on his lap. "Is it your arm? Do you need to see a doctor?"

"No, it's not that. I'm feeling strange, like things aren't right. I feel like I'm slipping into the Gladie Burger vortex."

"What the hell does that mean?"

Spencer rubbed his chest, as if it had grown tight and he was trying to loosen it. "I feel out of control, like I'm following you into a weird Gladie situation where donkeys fly."

I stood and put my hands on my hips. "Hey, I didn't make that donkey fly. That wasn't my fault."

Spencer looked to the left and sighed. "It's never your fault. You just fall into the Gladie vortex where crazy, horrible shit happens. And now the air is shifting..."

"That's the storm."

"No," he said. "It's not the storm. It's the vortex. The air shifted, and it's sucking me into your vortex."

I crossed my arms in front of me. "I don't have a vortex. The air shifted because of the storm. That's what you feel." Spencer shook his head, adamantly, which infuriated me. "There's literally a Wizard of Oz storm outside. Toto flew by. Scratch that. You'll be blaming me for Toto next."

"Well, do you have an alibi? Where were you when the tornado hit Dorothy's house?"

"Very funny." I stepped behind him and pushed his chair in the skinny woman's direction. "Gladie vortex. How about a Spencer vortex?" I mumbled to myself. "There's no such thing as a Gladie vortex. You can't blame me if people drop dead while I'm under the gas at the dentist's office or if I trip over a dead guy in the orchards. It could happen to anyone. It could happen to Laura Bush or Michelle Obama. The Pope. If it happened to the Pope, you wouldn't say there was a Pope vortex. Sheesh."

I stopped and sniffed the air. "Do you smell that?"

There was a strong smell of incense and a whole bunch of weed. "Oh, great," Spencer said, trying to adjust himself in the wheelchair despite his body cast. "The chief of police is getting a contact high."

Despite the smell of weed and the possible Gladie

vortex, we followed the skinny lady through double doors into a large ballroom-looking place, which turned out to be filled with beautiful fountains and a giant aquarium that covered the length and breadth of one wall. The aquarium held a large variety of fish, including sharks. There were about ten people in the room, half in velour track suits like the skinny lady's, and the other half in hospital gowns. The skinny lady had still not given us any details on Mrs. Friendly and there was no sign of the missing woman in the room.

Another crack of thunder shook the windows and flashes of lightning passed by them, but the generator held and the lights stayed on. As the sound dissipated, I heard the crackling of fire. Spencer pointed to a long, black strip on the floor that was glowing hot, like it was on fire.

"What on earth?" I asked out loud.

"Welcome to the integrative medicine's midnight health circle," one of the women in a track suit told me. I had never heard of a midnight health circle in a hospital. I wondered if "midnight health circle" was code for getting high. Weren't healthy pursuits usually in the morning?

I did another quick scan of the room, but didn't find Mrs. Friendly. The participants didn't seem like they were sick and half of them didn't seem like they wanted to be there. I didn't blame them. Back in their rooms, Stephen Colbert was on TV and the beds in the hospital were all memory foam. That was hard to give up and much better than a healing circle, whatever that was. I was only doing it because Mrs. Friendly might need help and because everyone thought I was loony tunes and I wanted to prove them wrong.

"Thank you," I told the woman who welcomed me. "Do you know if Mrs. Friendly is here?"

"I don't think I know her," she said. "Take your shoes off for the coals."

I sidestepped her and pushed Spencer toward the skinny lady who had promised me Mrs. Friendly. "Where's Mrs. Friendly?" I demanded. She didn't answer me. I was losing patience.

The skinny lady took her shoes off and the lights went off. The floor glowed brighter. "Wait a second. Coals? What did she mean by 'coals?'" I asked Spencer.

Spencer looked up at me with a scared puppy dog expression. His arm was at an angle in his cast, making him look vulnerable. "Vortex," he mouthed.

I took a deep breath and let it out, slowly. Spencer was right. I was a vortex of mishaps. I was danger-prone Gladie. "Take your shoes off," the skinny woman told me.

I looked down at my hospital-issued footy slippers with no-slip bottoms. "I'm not walking on hot coals," I said.

Spencer patted my back. "Good girl, Pinky. You're improving."

The coals had been placed in a long strip inside some kind of bin that protected the floor. The group formed a line behind me. Half seemed to share the skinny woman's positive outlook about walking barefoot across hot coals, but the other half wearing hospital gowns were shifting their weight from foot to foot, like they were ready to bolt. And not in the direction of the coals.

"Don't we need training for this?" one of the patients asked with more than a tinge of panic in his voice.

"Take deep breaths," one of the velour track suit ladies told him.

"What? Is that the training? Take deep breaths? Has anyone gotten burned doing this?"

"It's hot coals," Spencer told him, like that was answer enough.

"But there's a trick to it, right?" another patient asked.

"Not walking on them, probably," Spencer said, giving me a pointed look.

"I said I wasn't going to walk on them," I told him.

"I've done it a million times," the skinny woman said

and lifted her foot so everyone could see her perfect sole. "Let's get it done!" she announced and put her foot down.

I was no closer to finding Mrs. Friendly. I tapped the skinny woman's shoulder before she started her walk. "What about Mrs. Friendly? You said you knew Mrs. Friendly."

The skinny woman turned on me, and for the first time I noticed that her eyes didn't focus. Crazy eyes...I had seen them often since I moved to Cannes. I sighed. My lead had run into a dead end.

"We're all Mrs. Friendly!" the skinny woman announced, happily.

"We're all Mrs. Friendly, Pinky," Spencer repeated, looking straight at me.

I turned around to the next woman in a track suit. "Mrs. Friendly?"

"Never heard of her."

I looked down the line and was surprised to see my orderly. As I caught his eyes, he turned to help someone, but I got the impression that he was there for me. Watching me. I wanted to question him, too, but a young man in the corner started to play the Beatles' *Back in the USSR* on a sitar and the skinny woman skipped across the coals.

It was my turn, but I ducked out of the line, pulling

Spencer backward with me. The line moved forward with one participant after another skipping across the coals. At first, it looked like it was going to go off without a hitch, but then there was the inevitable screaming in agony.

"Sonofabitch!" one of them yelled.

"Deep breaths!" another yelled.

"My feet can't take deep breaths!"

"I'm on fire!"

One after another, healing circle participants ran for their lives across the coals.

The Midnight Healing Circle was brutal.

"We should probably get out of here," Spencer told me. I agreed with him. The vortex was closing in, and we needed to make room for the emergency services.

"They're probably fine," I said, as three people threw themselves down on the ground and clutched at their feet in pain.

"Skin grows back," Spencer said.

"Like hair," I said, thinking about Lucy.

Luckily, we were in a hospital. As we walked out, I looked back to see the orderly attending to some of the victims.

By the time we left the room, the loudspeaker was announcing a "Code Lavender," which I assumed had something to do with third-degree burns, because there was a group of doctors and nurses running through the lobby toward us.

"Have you ever heard of 'Code Lavender' before?" I asked Spencer. He looked up at me. His cheeks were distended and he was turning blue. "Are you holding your breath?" I asked. He nodded. "Why are you holding your breath?"

With his good hand, Spencer pointed away from the integrative medicine room. I pushed him to the elevator. He exhaled and then gulped air. "What was that about?" I asked.

"I didn't want to suck up any vortex air."

"I'm not sure I like this vortex talk. I didn't have anything to do with that in there."

He nodded. "I know. I know. But it's an aura thing, a force field around you."

"Like I'm a Jonah?" I asked.

He pointed at me. "Yes! Jonah. Thank you. I couldn't think of the name."

The elevator beeped and the doors opened. Dr. Fric stepped out with an older man.

"But we thought it was just heartburn," the man said, obviously concerned. Dr. Fric put his arm around his shoulders.

"Gallbladder," the doctor said, shaking his head. "I'll operate in the morning. She'll be fine and out of here in no time."

Spencer and I entered the elevator. I watched Dr. Fric walk away with the man, through the gap in the elevator doors as they closed. Something about Dr. Fric bothered me, but I couldn't figure out what.

"I heard they brought that doctor in from New York," Spencer told me, as the elevator went up to his floor. "He's supposed to be some kind of whiz kid. A real dynamo. I heard he operated on Giuliani and Clinton on the same day. 'Gold Fingers Fric,' that's what my nurse called him." Spencer yawned. "I think I'm done for tonight, Pinky. I'm sorry we didn't find your Mrs. Friendly, but it's probably for the best. A hallucination is so much better than what usually happens. If there was really a Mrs. Friendly, we'd be up all night searching for her and chasing after a bad guy who kidnaps old ladies with gallstones or something like that." He yawned again. "So, this is much better, right? Right? Why are you looking at me like that, Pinky?"

I wasn't looking at him. I was looking right past him. His words hit me hard, and not just because they were typical, insensitive boyfriend words. I couldn't let this go. I was going to search for Mrs. Friendly, even if it took all night. Grandma wouldn't stop if love was on the line, and I wasn't going to stop if a life was on the line. And besides, I couldn't stop. I was a gambler in Las Vegas with one last chip in my pocket. I was a coke addict with one last line to snort. I was Gladie Burger: Snooper, buttinski, nosy parker.

I was going to help Mrs. Friendly.

The elevator doors opened, but I pushed the button for my floor and the doors closed again. "What are you doing?" Spencer asked.

"I've never taken LSD, Spencer. I'm not having a flashback."

"Shit." Spencer locked eyes with me and then looked up at the ceiling. "Okay, fine. If I had fallen in love with the supermodel, she would have never eaten and pizza nights would have been lonely. So, I guess it's a tradeoff."

"What supermodel?"

The doors opened, and I pushed Spencer out. I made a beeline for the room where Mrs. Friendly and I ate barbecue. It was dark and I turned on the light. The room was empty and clean with no sign that it had ever been used.

"Smells good," Spencer said. "Barbecue."

As the word left Spencer's mouth, he caught my eyes and froze. "Barbecue," we repeated in unison.

I bolted toward the refrigerator and opened it. There on the second shelf was my box of leftovers. I took it out and handed it to Spencer.

"What's that written on it?" he asked.

"It's Greek for don't touch. Mrs. Friendly used to teach Greek."

The only sound was the refrigerator humming. But my brain was humming too and I would have bet money that Spencer's brain was doing the same. Finally, I had proof that Mrs. Friendly was real and I hadn't made her up. We looked down at Mrs. Friendly's doodle and let it sink in. I wasn't crazy. Mrs. Friendly was real.

Now that we knew I wasn't crazy, we had two bigger problems to deal with. First, we needed to find out where Mrs. Friendly was. Second, we had to find out why was the hospital was covering up her disappearance.

CHAPTER 9

My favorite part about being a matchmaker is the turning point. I know what you're thinking, bubeleh. You're thinking my favorite part should be the happy ending! Happy ending, shmappy ending. The turning point is better. It's that moment when love comes into the equation, where paths change, where you find out that you're going in an entirely different direction and you're happy about it. Also, I like that it's not the end. I like it better when we still have story left to go.

Lesson 64, Matchmaking advice from your
Grandma Zelda

"I'm going to call for back up," Spencer said in his best police chief voice. His authority was hampered by his plastered arm, which looked like it was frozen halfway to a salute. His mobility was hampered too. I could defy him and be reasonably sure that he couldn't stop me.

I mean, he couldn't physically stop me.

"Nice try," I said, scanning the room. "You're not getting backup. I'm backup. And frontup. I'm all of the ups." I found a set of scrubs draped on a chair. It was a perfect disguise for my plan to find Mrs. Friendly and take down whatever conspiratorial group I had discovered in the high-class hospital for the one-percent. I stripped off my gown and began to get dressed in the scrubs.

"Pinky," he said, his lips drawn in a tight line and his plastered arm pointing in my direction.

"Spencer."

He wagged his finger at me. "Let's find me a phone. I'm calling this in."

"Nice try," I repeated, tying the drawstring of the scrubs pants. "Remington is going to get the same run around that we got and we'll be nowhere again. I have a plan. I'm going undercover."

"What?"

My pulse raced with the excitement of a mystery. Mrs. Friendly was missing or worse and I was going to hunt down whoever was responsible for her disappearance. "The orderly and the nurse have to be in on it. I'm going to find out what they've been up to. Come on."

"Pinky, your eyes look like you've mainlined the entire country of Columbia. You're giddy."

"I wonder if the conspiracy stops with the orderly and the nurse," I said, ignoring him. "This could be bigger than Watergate." I looked off into the space behind Spencer, fantasizing about taking down the ring of old lady kidnappers.

I was raring to go. I grasped the handles of Spencer's wheelchair and began to push him toward the door, but he threw his feet down on the floor to brake.

"Just a minute. Just a minute," he growled. "I told you that I'm in charge. You're not in charge. Policeman in charge. Matchmaker not in charge. Me. Not you. Me. Not you. Am I getting through to you, Pinky?"

"No. Pick up your feet so we can get going. When you were in charge, you said I was having an LSD flashback. So, now I'm in charge."

"But…"

I opened the door and pulled him out, but stopped dead when I saw the orderly walking down the hallway toward us. "Duck! There's the orderly." I pulled the wheelchair back into the room and shut the door, with a soft click. "Don't give us away," I whispered to Spencer. "I hope he doesn't come in here."

"My kingdom for a phone," Spencer said. I shushed him. "I didn't even get leftover barbecue." My stomach rumbled in response. Leftover barbecue sounded delicious. My appendix was supposed to be making me feel sick, but besides a bloated belly and a wicked case of heartburn, I felt fine and was ready to choke down a cow's worth of BBQ.

But I wasn't allowed to eat before my surgery and time was ticking away for poor Mrs. Friendly, so there was no snacking for Spencer or me. After a minute, I opened the door a crack and peeped out. "The coast is clear," I whispered.

"Great. That's a relief." Spencer shook his fist at the ceiling. "Help, I've fallen in love with James Bond."

I opened the door all the way. "Come on, let's go."

My plan was to gather witnesses. Pretending to be a nurse, I could get the inside scoop. Then, I would decimate the people-- like the man in the hallway and Lucy's siblings-- for lying to me about Mrs. Friendly. Come to think of it, why did they lie? Could they have been in on the conspiracy, too?

I wheeled Spencer to the next room and parked him outside in the hallway. "I'll be right back. Wish me luck," I said, smoothing the scrubs and ducking inside the room.

A middle-aged man was lying in his bed, watching an

old Beverly Hillbillies episode on television. "There you are," he said to me. "I gotta go."

"Go where?"

"You know. Go. I gotta go. Help me to the crapper."

Oh, geez. I was pretty sure that Miss Marple never had to help anyone go to the crapper when she was on a case.

"I'm not that kind of nurse," I told him.

"What does that mean?" he grumbled.

"There are the crapper nurses and then there are the other kind of nurses." I fluffed his pillow to show him that I was the non-crapper kind of nurse.

He slapped my hand away. "Woman, if you don't help me to the crapper, you're going to have a big mess to deal with in this bed. You got me?"

I took a deep breath and blew it out slowly. "I got you," I said.

He took my left hand, and I lifted his torso up with my other arm. I got an eyeful of his old man butt as I helped him stand. "They say this is some kind of Rolls Royce hospital, but it doesn't change the fact that I have to crap," he said, shuffling toward the bathroom.

"I hear you. Hey, you know who else had to crap?

Mrs. Friendly. Do you know her?"

"What did you say?"

"A nice lady. Little round glasses. I haven't seen her for a while. Have you?"

We reached the bathroom door. He grabbed the knob and pulled himself forward. "Listen, lady, I can only hold onto these bowels for so long."

I closed the door behind him to give him privacy. "So, have you seen her?" I asked through the door.

"Sounds familiar. A pain in the ass like you, right?"

"Yes! That's the one."

There were some groaning and pushing noises. "She asked a lot of questions."

"What kind of questions?"

The toilet flushed and the man opened the door. "About the hospital. About the people who worked here and the patients and why they were here. Why? What's it to you?"

I helped him back to his bed. "I'm looking for her and thought maybe you knew where she is."

"All I know is that I need a new pacemaker and I was promised three weather channels, but there's only two. Hand me the clicker, will you?"

I handed it to him and he changed the station. On television, they were predicting the end of the world for everyone living in a twenty-mile radius of Cannes. "Hm. Tornado warning," the man said.

"We don't get tornados."

"Looks like we are tonight. I hope the tornadoes blow away half of the town's population. They let in all kinds these days. Gives the town a bad smell."

I was probably part of the town that smelled bad, and I should have been insulted, but I had finally gotten a real lead on Mrs. Friendly and I wasn't going to let go. "So, what exactly was she asking about?"

"I don't know. She wanted to know about my pacemaker and how long I needed one and who was doing the operation. Stuff like that. Why do you want to know? Don't you have people to check on? Why are you wearing no-slip footies? Are nurses wearing those these days?"

My cover was getting blown. I sucked at being a spy. I needed to leave before he called a real nurse. "All righty, then. I guess I'll be going. There's a woman down the hall with bunions that need rubbing."

I backed out of the room. Down the hall, Nurse Millie was wheeling a bed into a room. On the bed was a person wrapped in bandages with only slits for eyes. Luckily the nurse's attention was focused on her patient and she didn't seem to notice me.

Then it hit me. Spencer's wheelchair was parked where I had left it outside of the crapper man's room, but there was no sign of Spencer.

My hand flew to my mouth and I stifled a loud gasp. I had lost Spencer. He had wanted to call for backup, but I wouldn't let him and now he had vanished. He had disappeared like Mrs. Friendly. Instead of finding one person, I had lost another one.

I bit my knuckle as terror flooded me. There was a loud crack of thunder and the hospital shook. It was the end of the world, people were disappearing, and I was all alone with a bad appendix and no-slip footies.

Down the hall, the door closed. I looked from it to Spencer's chair and back again, and a niggling suspicion creeped up my spine. Then, the door to the room down the hall opened again and Millie stepped out. I plastered my body to the wall so she wouldn't see me. The moment she turned the corner, I tip-toed down the hall. I opened the door a half of an inch and peeked in. The coast was clear. Making sure that no one was coming, I opened the door all the way and walked inside.

The room was dark, so I turned on the light. On the

bed was a person wrapped like a mummy. My eyes filled up with tears. "Spencer, is that you?" I whispered, my voice cracking with emotion. I approached the bed and studied the wrapped body, trying to look through the eye slits, searching for Spencer's baby blues.

But I couldn't see anything. "Spencer? Is that you? Did I do this to you? I'm terrible backup." Tears flowed and dripped onto his chest. "Sorry about that," I said and wiped his chest dry. "Wait a second. When did you grow breasts?"

I patted his chest and, sure enough, he had large, floppy breasts. I pulled the sheets down. Even wrapped from head to toe, this person was definitely a woman and about five-feet-tall. It wasn't Spencer. Spencer was about six-foot-two with a large body cast and pecks that you could crack walnuts on.

The person in the bed had Mrs. Friendly's exact shape.

"Mrs. Friendly?" I whispered. "Is that you? What did they do to you?"

I was horrified for her, but ecstatic that I found her. At least, I was relatively certain it was her. She didn't answer me. She didn't even moan or snore and, as far as I could tell, she wasn't breathing.

Uh oh.

Poor Mrs. Friendly.

I was about to climb on her chest and give her CPR, when I heard voices outside. I opened the door a crack and peeked out. The voices were coming closer. I hopped out of the room and ducked into the next one. With the door open slightly, I watched the nurse and the orderly go back into Mrs. Friendly's room.

I shut the door of the room I had snuck into. I rested my forehead on the wall and tried to make sense of what was happening. Poor Mrs. Friendly was wrapped like a mummy in the next room. She could have been dead or alive, but something definitely bad had happened to her and Nurse Millie and the orderly were responsible, or, at the very least, they knew what happened to her and were covering it up. They had lied to me and pretended that Mrs. Friendly didn't exist. They had made me feel like I had been going crazy.

My stomach cramped, reminding me that in only a few hours I was going to have an operation. I didn't have a lot of time to shine the light on the evil happening at West Side Hospital.

Damn it. I needed backup.

Where was Spencer when I needed him? Was he hurt? Did Nurse Millie get him? Did he get tired of the Gladie vortex and escape out into the storm of the century, preferring to make his way in a hospital gown, body cast, and no-slip footies through tornadoes rather than deal with me?

"May I help you?" a voice behind me asked. I turned around. A man was lying in bed, and he was about forty years old. A small light shined over his head.

I gasped and stepped back. "Is that…?" I stammered, pointing at his head.

"An arrow in my head? Yes, it is. Darnedest thing, right?"

I put my hand on the side of my head, as if I expected an arrow to hit me in the temple, too. "Do you need help? Should I call someone?"

"Nope. I'm fine. I was given the good juice." He patted the IV machine next to him.

"But your, your…" I stammered, pointing at his head.

"My head? The arrow? They're taking it out tomorrow. Something about waiting for the whosits and whatsits in my head to calm their horses before they can remove it. I'm just supposed to stay calm and not move around a lot. Amazing that I can talk, right?" I nodded. "It doesn't even hurt. Itches a little, though. My wife is going to put me up on YouTube. She says I'm going to be famous. She was calling me Arrow, but that's already the name of a superhero, and there's a trademark issue, so…"

I nodded, again.

"Did you need something? Did you want to take my temperature?" he asked.

"What?"

"Temperature? Blood pressure?"

I looked down at my scrubs and remembered that I was pretending to be a nurse. "Uh," I said.

"Maybe you could fluff my pillow," he suggested.

"You mean the pillow under your head?" He stared at me as if he was trying to figure out how to answer my question or wondering if he got the worst nurse in history. "Of course under your head," I said, covering my tracks.

"I don't know why, but my neck is stiff," he said, as I tried to adjust his pillow without shaking his head or bumping the arrow. It was a hunter's kind of arrow with blue and white feathers at one end. The arrow was sticking out about a foot from the man's head. The least they could have done was to saw it down to a reasonable length, but maybe they were afraid of jostling it. One false move, and the man could have been a drooling vegetable, licking car antennas or whatever one licks when a chunk of brain has been arrowed.

It was all I could do not to throw up, while I adjusted his pillow. "Easy does it," he said. I was working up a thick flop sweat that dripped down on his bed. Finally, I got it adjusted, and he was still alive and talking in full sentences.

"There you go," I said. "You probably don't need anything else, right?"

He didn't have time to answer. The door opened, and I jumped, knocking the man's pillow with my hip. The man screamed and scooted out of my reach.

"There you are. I thought I heard you," Spencer said, barging into the room. He was still wearing his body cast and hospital gown, but he had figured out how to walk in it, even though his arm was still locked in a half salute.

"Where did you go?" I demanded. "I thought you were dead or kidnapped or running away from…you know."

"From you? From the vortex?"

"Take that back. There's no vortex. Where did you go? What were you doing?"

"I was calling for backup, or at least I tried," Spencer explained. "The storm brought down the phone lines and it must have gotten the cell towers, too. I couldn't even find a CB radio. So, it's just us. You, me, and the vortex."

"Stop with the vortex, Spencer."

"Fine. There's no vortex. Happy? Oh,

my...Sonofabitch!"

At first I thought he was yelling at me, but his attention was elsewhere. Spencer had noticed the arrow in the man's head. He pointed at him with his mouth open and horror plastered on his face.

"Pinky, what did you do? What did you do?"

"I resent that," I said. "I didn't do anything."

Spencer grabbed my arm. "It's okay. It's okay. We'll say it was self-defense. But an arrow? How could you with an arrow?"

I shrugged out of his grasp. "I didn't do that."

"No, she didn't," the man with the arrow in his head said. "It's a funny story, actually. You won't believe this."

Spencer blinked. "You can talk? You're alive?"

"Crazy, right?" the man said.

"Spencer this is Arrow," I said.

"The superhero?" Spencer asked.

"See? It's going to be a problem," the man said.

"He's having it taken out tomorrow," I explained.

Spencer nodded and put his hand out to shake.

"Sorry," Arrow said. "I can't shake your hand or it will jostle the you-know-what."

"Oh, sorry." Spencer took his hand back. "I didn't mean to jostle you."

"Not to be inhospitable, but what are you doing here?" the man asked, reasonably.

"Well…" Spencer and I said in unison. I had no idea what to say. I didn't think he would believe that I was hiding from the staff, who I believed had kidnapped and killed an old woman and had wrapped her up like a mummy and stuck her in the next room. But what did I know? I mean, the man had an arrow in his head. After that, pretty much any story was believable.

"I was looking for my keys," Spencer said. My head whipped around toward him in surprise. For a chief of police, I thought he could have come up with a better excuse than his keys. Spencer shrugged. "I panicked," he whispered.

"We're leaving now," I told the man with the arrow in his head. He seemed relieved at this news.

Before I could open the door, it was thrust open and a tall man dressed all in black with a black ski mask over his head burst in. He held a knife in his hand, and he lifted it over his head and ran after me.

In moments of extreme danger, it's normal that the

flight or fight response kicks in. Would-be victims either run like hell or stand and fight, some so filled with adrenaline that they get super strength and can lift cars.

But when I was faced with a maniacal killer, hell-bent on stabbing me to death, I didn't lift a car and I didn't pull an Usain Bolt. In fact, I might not have even possessed a flight or fight response. I was responseless.

I just stood in place and didn't even scream. My no-slip footies were rooted to the floor, while I watched my attacker come at me. Right before his knife made contact with my face, however, Spencer's fight or flight response kicked in and he fought like the Muhammad Ali of men in body casts and hospital gowns.

Forgetting that his left arm was in a cast and secured to his torso, he let fly with a left hook. The cast held firm, but the momentum took over, sending Spencer through the air, his body off-balance. The attacker was focused on killing me, so he had no idea he was about to be pulverized by Spencer.

With the added weight of the body cast, Spencer made quite an impact. He collided with the attacker with a loud crack. The knife flew out of the attacker's hand It sailed through the air, knocking the wall behind me and clanging to the floor. The attacker pushed Spencer off of him, but Spencer was like a dog with a bone. He punched the attacker with his good hand, aiming for his face, but the attacker turned and Spencer hit him on the side of the head. This time, they both went down.

As they fell, they grabbed onto each other, as if they were trying to catch their balance, but it didn't work. They fell sideways and landed on the bed on poor Arrow's legs.

"This isn't happening!" Arrow shouted, which was exactly my thinking.

I couldn't believe it was happening, either. I watched as the man with the arrow in his head tried to remain motionless while two grown men wrestled on the lower half of his body. Arrow and I exchanged looks. It was like watching a train chug closer to a damsel in distress who was tied to the tracks. It was just a matter of seconds before Spencer and the attacker jostled the man enough so that the arrow did its thing in his brain. Licking car antennas was definitely in his future.

Worrying about his brain got my brain to get my feet to move. I picked up the knife from the floor and wielded it over Spencer and the attacker, trying to aim. They rolled around, making it hard to get a clear path to the attacker. I didn't want to stab Spencer, but he was having a difficult time battling the attacker with only one working arm. At first, he got some good shots in, but then the attacker pinned his right arm. Spencer was helpless, relying on throwing his weight against the attacker.

WEST SIDE GORY

"Why is this happening?" Arrow asked.

It was now or never. I had to help Spencer, or we would all be goners: Spencer, me, and the man with the arrow in his head.

CHAPTER 10

Remember this, bubeleh: Underpants. Always wear them. Even in the shower…wear your underpants. Okay. Okay. That was a little joke. Don't wear your underpants in the shower. But for the love of God, wear them everywhere else. And not those fakakta thong underpants. Those aren't real. I don't understand why anyone wants to walk around with a strip of nylon wedged up their tuchus. Kinky is fine, but nylon up your tuchus isn't fine. So, don't let your matches go out without underpants. That goes for men, too. Commandos are only good in the army. Nobody wants a commando under a gabardine trouser. You got me?

Lesson 80, Matchmaking advice from your
Grandma Zelda

"I don't like this," the man with the arrow in his head

said. "I don't understand why this is happening."

Him and me both. The attacker and Spencer were going at it like it was the annual wedding dress sale at Bloomies and there was only one mermaid dress left in stock. The attacker was strong and Spencer was stuck in a body cast, but Spencer made a valiant effort. He knocked the attacker with his plaster cast, making an *oomph* noise, each time he made contact.

But there was only one way this fight could go. There was no way Spencer could win and poor Arrow's YouTube video would be of his funeral. I had to help. With the knife in my hand, I waited for my chance. Finally, I got a clear shot. I held the knife over my head, ready to impale the attacker in the back.

The image of the knife's sharp edge sinking into the attacker's flesh flashed through my mind. Blech. I couldn't stab him, even if he was about to kill us all. Even though I didn't think I could stab him, I was pretty sure I could bludgeon him to death. I turned the knife and pounded the man's head with the broadside.

I hit him three times, but it had little effect. He looked up to see who was hitting him, and Spencer took advantage of that moment to free his good arm. He punched the attacker repeatedly with a hammer fist, knocking him off the bed. Spencer struggled to get up and I grabbed his arm to help him.

By the time Spencer was standing again, the attacker had fled the room, and I could hear his shoes on the floor as he ran away. I listened until I couldn't hear him anymore.

"Am I alive? Am I alive?" the man with the arrow in his head asked.

"I think so?" I said like a question.

"Testing one, two, three. Istanbul was once Constantinople. Suzy sells seashells by the seashore. Okay. Okay. I'm all right."

"Are *you* all right?" I asked Spencer. His body cast had a crack in it, but it was still functional. He had a bloody nose, and his perfect hair was disheveled. His hospital gown had opened, giving me a good look at his nakedness. I gave him a once-over for stab wounds, but he was fine.

I sniffed. I had almost lost Spencer. That fact hit me like a ton of bricks. I didn't want to lose him. I wanted him around me for a long time. Perhaps forever. I didn't want to lose him when I had just found him.

I dropped the knife, threw my arms around his neck, and pulled him in for a kiss. I had a ferocious need and I kissed him like he was trying to get away.

But he wasn't trying to get away. He met my kiss with

his own need, pressing his lips against mine, thrusting his tongue into my mouth. His good hand traveled down my back to my butt, which he caressed like it was trying to get away, too.

"I don't understand what's happening," the man with the arrow in his head said.

I knew that we had to stop, that we weren't alone, that we were in a man's hospital room, that we had just been attacked, that I had a bum appendix, and that Spencer was in a body cast.

I also knew that Spencer's gown was open, and he was very happy to see me.

But I kept kissing him because I couldn't stop. It was like eating potato chips. There was no stopping until the bag was empty.

Or when the door opened, and Dr. Fric, Nurse Millie, and the orderly burst in.

"I don't mean to complain, but I want a new nurse," the man with the arrow in his head said.

"What's going on here?" Dr. Fric demanded. His eyes darted to Spencer's lower half and then returned to my face. Quickly, I re-tied Spencer's gown for him.

"You!" I shouted, pointing at Millie and the orderly.

"You took Mrs. Friendly!"

"Not this again," Millie said. "I think we need to sedate her, Doctor."

I put my hands on my hips and stomped a foot on the floor. "I do not need to be sedated. I'm perfectly calm. But you need to be arrested. I know what you did to Mrs. Friendly."

"Concussion, Doctor," Millie told him.

Dr. Fric waved his hands in the air. "Let's all calm down. What are you two doing in this room? You've woken half of the hospital. and you've upset Mr. Hood. He's not supposed to move until his surgery tomorrow morning."

"Hood like Robin Hood?" Spencer asked, and we looked at him.

"Crazy coincidence, right?" the man with the arrow in his head said.

"I'm going to have to ask you to leave, immediately," the doctor said in his sternest doctor voice.

"No. First, they have to explain about Mrs. Friendly," I said. "I found her next door," I explained to Spencer. "They've got her wrapped up like a mummy. I don't know if she's alive or dead."

"That's ridiculous," the nurse sneered. "That's the new patient that came in this evening, Doctor."

"The accident? A bad case," the doctor said, shaking his head, like he was upset that the patient had to suffer.

"I'm telling you that it's Mrs. Friendly. Same size. Same height." I turned to Spencer. "Same boobs, too," I whispered.

"Doctor, Gladie and I found proof that Mrs. Friendly did exist. Gladie didn't make her up," Spencer said. "But more importantly, we were just attacked. A man in black attacked us with a knife."

"Now I've heard everything," the nurse said, rolling her eyes. I wanted to slap the eyes out of her head.

"There's the knife," Spencer said.

"There was a man. He jostled my arrow," the man with the arrow in his head said. "I want to go to the other hospital. They don't have jacuzzi tubs in the bathrooms, but…"

"Let's bring this conversation out of Mr. Hood's room. Shall we?" the doctor said.

He opened the door and we filed out. "Sorry about everything," I told the man with the arrow in his head as I left. "It was nice to meet you."

The hallway was full of patients who had gotten up to see what the ruckus was about. Lucy was among them and, when she spotted me, she smiled and sauntered over. She was wearing a peach peignoir with fur topped slippers. Her head was covered in one of her headpieces, and she seemed relaxed, probably sedated up to her eyeballs.

"I figured it was you, darlin'," she said when she reached me. "It sounded like someone was being murdered and I thought: 'well Gladie has to be somewhere around that party.'"

"Everyone back to your room," Dr. Fric commanded. "Nothing to see here. It was just the storm making itself known, but all's well. So, please go back to your rooms."

It took a couple minutes, but finally the patients shuffled away, most of them taking looks behind them in the hopes, probably, of seeing something juicy.

Dr. Fric was having none of the juicy stuff. He corralled us into Mrs. Friendly's room and closed the door. "What's going on?" Lucy asked me in a whisper. She had stayed with me to see what was what.

"A woman went missing, but Cruella and Pugsley said she never existed and tried to make it look like I was crazy. Meanwhile, Spencer and I looked for her, but were attacked by a man with a knife."

Lucy slapped her thigh. "Damn those tranquilizers. They knocked me out and I missed the fun. What's happening now?"

I pointed at Mrs. Friendly. "That's her. That's the missing woman."

"The stiff in the mummy suit?"

I chewed on my bottom lip. "I hope she's not a stiff."

"Is this who you say is Mrs. Friendly?" the doctor asked me.

"Yes. That's her and those two did this to her."

The nurse pushed some buttons on the computer next to the bed and showed it to the doctor. "See? This is the accident patient."

He studied the chart on the computer for a moment and returned to us. "Everything looks on the up and up."

"But…" I said.

He put his hand on my shoulder in his best Marcus Welby pose and tried to calm me down. "I promise that I'll check this out, but there are patients' rights of privacy that I can't cross. We shouldn't even be in this room. But I promise you—promise—that I will look into this and make sure. Okay?"

"If you could just unwrap her a little, I could tell you."

The nurse made a can-you-believe-this-woman sound.

"We can't do that," the doctor explained in his serene tone. "But I promise you that I will look into this whole matter."

"Gladie always knows when mischief is being played," Lucy said, coming to my rescue. "If she says that that's Mrs. Friendly, then that's Mrs. Friendly, and if she says these two are no account, scheming, liar kidnappers, well, then that's exactly what they are."

"Thank you," I mouthed to her.

"We have a bigger problem here," Spencer said. "I'm the Cannes Chief of Police. We were attacked. This hospital has to be locked down immediately. There's a dangerous man on the loose."

"Of course," the doctor said, taking that announcement more seriously than a kidnapped old lady. "Right away. Come with me to security."

"What about Mrs. Friendly?" I asked.

"I'll take the chief to security and come back and investigate this further. Meanwhile, you need to go back to bed. Doctor's orders. You have surgery in the morning."

"You do?" Lucy asked me.

"Appendix," I said, touching the left side of my belly. It was still bloated, and my heartburn hadn't gone away.

The doctor asked the orderly to escort me back to my room, but I refused to go anywhere with him. He was in on the conspiracy, as far as I was concerned.

"I'll take her," Lucy offered, and the doctor accepted. He went with Spencer to security, and the nurse and the orderly stayed with poor Mrs. Friendly. I hadn't given up on her, but I knew when I was outnumbered. Like Sun Tzu said in the "Art of War," when there's too many troops, fall back and attack when they're not looking. Actually, I had never read The Art of War but I figured there had to be something like that in there.

"Don't get into trouble," Spencer said, giving me a peck on the cheek. "I'll be back as soon as possible. Have Lucy stay with you. Don't take candy from strangers. Don't walk under any ladders. Don't open an umbrella indoors. Don't..."

I put my hand up. "Okay. I get it. I'll lock myself in my bathroom until you get back."

He kissed my cheek, again. "Good girl."

Lucy walked down the hall with me toward the elevator. "Your appendix is on the other side, you know," she said.

"Not mine."

"But…"

"I've got to help Mrs. Friendly."

Lucy looked at one of her perfectly manicured fingernails. "Oh, honey. I knew the second I laid eyes on you in the hallway that you had the murder bug in you. You have a tiger by the tail and nothing will make you let it go. So, how can I help? I want to hold a tiger's tail, too."

I gave her the full rundown of what had happened since I woke up in the hospital. I explained about Mrs. Friendly and the leftover Bobby Flay food, how the nurse and the orderly said she never existed, along with the man in the hallway and Lucy's sister and brother.

Lucy stopped walking and put her hand on the wall for support. "You mean to tell me that my worthless no account sister and brother didn't have your back?"

"To be fair, they had eighty proof running through their veins." But that was being more generous than I felt. I wanted to kill Cletus and Earlene for saying they never met Mrs. Friendly.

"Let's get 'em," Lucy said, her eyes focused on something in the far distance.

"Excuse me?"

"How dare they treat my best friend and maid of honor this way! I'm going to fry them a new egg, if you know what I mean."

I had no idea what she meant, but she didn't stay to explain herself. She practically skipped away in her fancy, fur slippers and pushed the elevator call button. I caught up to her just as the doors opened.

When we got to the next floor, the doors opened and Lucy stomped out, ready to do damage. Then I saw the man in the hallway, the one with his legs wide apart, still doing laps.

I waved, and his mouth dropped open. "Oh, nooooo," he said, gingerly making a tight U-turn and heading in the opposite direction.

"Get him!" I yelled. I must have temporarily lost my mind, or I was fed up with the conspiracy, or Lucy's kill 'em attitude was contagious. Either way, I was bound and determined to get the truth out, even if I had to fry him a new egg.

Lucy bounded into action. She ran past me with her peach gown flowing behind her. "Stop or I'll shoot!" she yelled.

The man stopped and flattened his back against the

wall.

Lucy got in his face, sticking her finger under his nose. "Why were you running?"

"Because you were chasing! Are you going to shoot me?"

Lucy shot me a look. "Should we shoot him?"

We didn't have a gun. I wasn't packing iron in my no-slip footies. But I didn't let him know that. "Why did you deny seeing Mrs. Friendly?" I demanded.

"This again? I told you that I don't want to get involved. I refuse to talk to the police or the press," he said and winced.

"What's the matter with you?" Lucy asked. "Why are you standing like that?"

"You didn't say you didn't want to get involved before," I said. "You said you never saw her. Is that it? You didn't want to get involved?"

"Please, you don't understand. I was guaranteed complete privacy."

Lucy's face brightened. "Keep going, Gladie. I think you got a hot one. Open this box and let it fly."

Sometimes I had no idea what Lucy was talking

about, but this time I caught the gist. "So you do remember her," I said to the man.

"Why do you want privacy?" Lucy asked. "Whatcha got? Herpes? What?" The man flinched and looked down at his crotch. "I think I'm close, Gladie."

I was pretty sure I didn't want to know why he was looking at his crotch and why he wanted privacy. All I cared about was Mrs. Friendly. "Are you part of the conspiracy? Keeping secrets with Nurse Millie?"

"What? Who?"

"And the orderly?"

He shook his head. "No. No. I just didn't want to be pestered. Is that so much to ask?"

Lucy barked a laugh. "With Gladie Burger? Are you kidding? No chance. Way too much to ask. Tell him, Gladie. Pester him until he talks."

"Spill," I growled.

"Fine. Yes. I saw the old bat with you. Are you happy? Are you happy?"

I was ecstatic.

"Why did you lie?" I asked him.

"Because you went bat shit crazy, talking about the police. Nobody's supposed to know I'm here."

Lucy gasped and clutched her chest. "Why? Are you a spy?" She and I leaned forward so we wouldn't miss a word of his answer.

"Of course I'm not a spy. What's wrong with you people? I had a…" He mumbled the rest.

"What was that? Did you get that, Gladie?"

"I think I heard something about a totem."

"That doesn't make sense," Lucy complained. "How does that make sense?"

"Not totem," the man said. "Scrotum. I had a scrotum lift and new buttocks."

Lucy and I took a step back. "You got both sides covered?" Lucy asked.

"Hey, it's a new world out there. If you don't have thirty-year old balls, you're nothing. If you tell anybody about this, I'll sue your asses."

With the cat out of the bag, he continued walking, his legs wide apart like before. I threw up my hands in defeat. "That explains it, then," I told Lucy. "No conspiracy. Could all of the explanations be that simple?"

She shook her head. "No. Cletus wouldn't care who knew if he got a scrotum lift."

"Do you think that's true about the thirty-year old balls?"

"I don't know. In my previous line of work, I saw all kinds of balls. I could have carried groceries with a few of them."

As we walked to Cletus and Earlene's room, I tried to fit all of the pieces of the mystery in my mind. Who was Mrs. Friendly? She had told me that she had gallstones and she was true to her Friendly name. The old man who I helped to the crapper had told me that Mrs. Friendly asked a lot of questions about the staff and about his illness. Was that some kind of clue? It didn't sound like one to me. Was there really a conspiracy, or was the story bigger? Could Mrs. Friendly have something embarrassing like a scrotum lift that she didn't want to divulge? Could the nurse and the orderly have been trying to preserve her privacy and that's why they lied to me? Was the conspiracy just a matter of people trying to get me to mind my own business?

It would have been a possibility, but what about the man in black, wielding the knife? He had gone after me first. A knife was a little over the top to try and get me to mind my own business.

No, something was happening at West Side Hospital

and it wasn't just scrotum lifts.

Lucy threw the door open to Cletus and Earlene's room. "I'm gonna whup your butts!" she announced and walked in.

A noise to my left caught my attention, and I let the door close in front of me to check it out. "Psst," I heard. Nurse Millie was standing in the shadows down the hallway. She crooked her finger at me. "Psst!" she called.

My skin prickled and fear crept up my spine. It wouldn't be smart to go to her, alone. She was probably responsible for the kidnapping of a little old lady, and she might have been in cahoots with a knife-wielding madman. In fact, she might be distracting me, and the knife-wielder could have been lying in wait for me.

Yes, it would be stupid to go to her, I thought, as she crooked her finger at me. It would be really, really stupid.

I walked toward her.

CHAPTER 11

In love, it's important to be brave. Take the step.
Thinking's all well and good, but bravery trumps thinking every
time. Sometimes, it's good to leap before you look.

Lesson 54, Matchmaking advice from your
Grandma Zelda

As I walked toward her, Millie looked from side to side, as if she was looking to see if someone was coming. She had changed from the in-control, put-together nurse, and now she was a bundle of nerves, chewing on a hangnail. When I got near, she grabbed my arm and pulled me close.

"I need to talk to you," she hissed.

"What did you do to Mrs. Friendly?"

"Shut up and listen. This thing is out of control. I didn't sign up for this."

"For what? For what?" Finally, I was getting somewhere. The nurse was going to spill. I was giddy with the thrill I only got right before a mystery was going to be solved. It was better than sex. Well, it was better than sex with anybody except for Spencer. Sex with Spencer was like solving a mystery while eating a jar of Nutella and getting a foot massage.

"I don't have a lot of time. If they catch me talking to you, I'm dead."

I leaned in closer. "Who? Who? Who will catch you talking to me?"

"I just went along with it for the money. Everyone needs money, right?"

I nodded. I always needed money. I bought toilet paper from a guy on a corner with no nose.

"What did you do for the money?" I asked her.

"But they didn't stop there," she continued. "And I can't be a part of it."

"Who's they? Didn't stop where? A part of what?" I was getting nowhere. I would have failed interrogation 101 at Gitmo. Barbara Walters would be ashamed of me.

"Listen, you need to help me. You have friends in high places."

"I do?"

"That Smythe woman and the Chief of Police."

"Oh, I guess I do," I said. I never thought of them that way. They were successful, but I lived with my grandmother, and my favorite bra was held together with two safety pins.

"Get me out of this jam. I'll rat everyone out."

"Everyone? Everyone who?"

"But I'm not going down for this. I'm not spending my life in prison because of them." Her eyes had gotten big with the stress of contemplating a life in prison.

"What did they do? What did you do? A life in prison? For what?"

"Get your boyfriend to cut me a deal and then I'll talk," she said, looking behind me. "Don't trust no one. No one. You understand me?"

I put a finger up. "When you say, don't trust no one, what do you mean?"

"And help Mrs. Friendly before it's too late."

I struggled to swallow. "Before it's too late?"

Millie wasn't listening. She was looking behind me and she was scared. I turned around to see what she was looking at. Spencer was marching toward me in his hospital gown and his beat up body cast. I was relieved to see him, not only because he was hotter than hell and believed in ladies first when it came to orgasms, but also because he was a trained law enforcement official and could get Millie to talk. I crooked my finger at him, like Millie had done to me, and pointed behind me. Spencer looked at me, questioningly.

"Millie," I explained, but when I turned around, she was gone. "The nurse was here," I told him.

Spencer scowled at me. "You were supposed to go straight to your room. Where's Lucy? Nobody listens to me. I'm the Chief of Police, you know. There's a lunatic with a knife wandering around this hospital and you're hanging out like you don't have a care in the world. Hey, why are you looking at me like that? Pinky? Pinky? You're scaring me."

I poked his chest. "I was talking. I was saying something important about the nurse." I stormed off to Cletus and Earlene's room. Spencer followed me.

"Fine. What did she say?"

"Oh, sure. Now you're interested."

"Gladys…" he growled.

"Don't call me Gladys."

"Well, tell me what she said."

I grabbed the door handle. "Like you care."

I opened the door and walked in. Lucy was reading Cletus and Earlene the riot act. She stopped when Spencer and I entered. "Tell them!" she ordered her siblings.

Cletus turned over in his bed, but Earlene sat up in hers and looked sheepish. "Go on," Lucy insisted.

"What's going on?" Spencer asked.

"We're sorry," Earlene said.

"Shut up," Cletus said. "You're going to ruin it for us."

"Ruin what?" I asked.

Lucy kicked Earlene's bed. "Tell her."

"They were going to give me free liposuction and Cletus was going to get dental implants," Earlene said.

"Excuse me?" Spencer asked.

He didn't understand, but I did. Cletus and Earlene had been bribed to keep quiet about Mrs. Friendly. It was easy to figure out who did that. Nurse Millie had been the one to talk to them before I questioned them about her. She must have made them the deal while I had waited outside of their room. Cletus and Earlene sold me out for liposuction and new teeth. It wasn't much, but people had sold out for less.

"It was the nurse who bribed you, right?" I asked.

"Yes, and the young guy," Earlene said.

Spencer caught my eye. "The orderly," he said, catching on.

"You two aren't worth a pig's butt in a chair convention," Lucy told them, which seemed to shame them. I had had enough. I wasn't any closer to helping Mrs. Friendly, but I was a notch closer to losing hope for humanity.

"I'm ready to go to my room," I told Spencer.

His expression softened. "Come on, Pinky. I'll tuck you in."

He put his good arm around me and we went back out into the hallway. It was the middle of the night and the storm was still raging. I only had a few hours before my surgery.

"I don't want to have an operation," I told Spencer.

"I'll be there when you wake up and I'll give you ice cream until you feel better."

"I like ice cream." I leaned my head on his chest. "Did you find the guy with the knife?"

"No, and it's strange. Not only are the phones out, but the hospital's emergency communication system is down."

"That's not normal?"

"That's not normal. I think this Mrs. Friendly business is bigger than we thought, which leads me to ask what the nurse had to tell you."

"She said…"

A couple nurses walked by and I shut up. Spencer pulled me into a nearby closet and closed us in. It smelled like bleach. We stood chest to body cast, and I looked up into his beautiful blue eyes. He adjusted his body. I remembered that he was uncomfortable in his cast and should have been resting.

"Tell me," he said.

"She wanted me to convince you to cut her a deal."

"*You* are going to convince *me*?"

I shrugged. "She said she wouldn't spill the beans until you did. She said what you said: this is bigger than we know. She was given money to do whatever she did. And she told me to save Mrs. Friendly."

"Damn it. I picked a great time to be in a body cast."

"Yeah, you did." I didn't think it was the moment to remind him that I was to blame for his body cast. But he had a point. Without backup from the police force, we were down to half of a Spencer. "What about the security guards? They could help us."

"I don't know who to trust."

"That's what Millie said. She said, 'don't trust no one.'"

"Damn it."

"You got me, though. You can trust me."

Spencer smirked and drew his finger along my lower lip. "I got you?" he asked, but didn't wait for an answer. He pushed me up against the shelves of cleaning supplies. He palmed my breast, making me gasp in pleasure. "You're making that hospital gown work for me," he said, his voice deep and gravely.

I knew that voice. It was the voice that said we were about to get it on. I didn't know how we were going to get it on in a broom closet with him in a body cast, but Spencer was pretty industrious where his penis was concerned. He already had my gown up around my middle and was

190

reacquainting himself with my nether regions.

"Ohhhhh," I moaned.

"Moan again for me, Pinky."

"Ohhhhh," I moaned again, but it wasn't because his fingers were doing a tour of my erogenous zones. My appendix took that moment to decide to explode in my body. At least it felt like it was exploding. "Ohhh!"

I pushed Spencer off of me and I doubled over in pain. "I'm dying. I'm dying," I moaned.

"What did I do?"

"It's my appendix. Oh my God, I'm dying. What should I do?"

"I never made a woman's appendix burst before."

I looked up at Spencer. He was smiling, pleased as punch that his magic Don Juan ability had made one of my organs explode.

"Are you kidding me?" I said. "Look at you. I'm dying here, you know. I need a doctor. I need surgery."

"Okay. Okay," he said, helping me up. "Let's get you to a doctor. It looks like your operation will be moved up."

"But Mrs. Friendly…"

"You're my priority. Let's get going."

I took a step and my body let loose a loud, long fart. It sounded like a cross of a foghorn and a cow giving birth.

"Oh, wow," I said.

"Oh, wow is right. It's a shame we didn't record that. You could have been in the Book of World Records. And it drowned out the bleach smell. Doesn't this room have some kind of ventilation? Shit, what did you eat today?"

"No," I said. "I mean, oh, wow, I feel much better now."

"Are you sure? You were dying a second ago."

I took stock of my body. My belly wasn't bloated anymore, my heartburn was gone, and I didn't have any pain. I pushed on the left side of my belly. Nope. No pain.

"The fart cured my appendix," I said.

Spencer arched an eyebrow. "I don't have a medical degree, but I'm reasonably sure that farts don't cure appendicitis. Are you sure you're okay?"

"Never better. I could go for some pizza."

"My girlfriend, ladies and gentlemen."

"Where were we?" I asked. "Were we making out, or

figuring out how to save Mrs. Friendly?"

Spencer sniffed. "It smells like bleach-flavored farts in here. I never went out with a woman who farted before."

"I can assure you that every woman you dated farted at some point. It was probably an anorexic, kale-smelling fart, so you didn't realize it happened. And a fart squeezing through one of those tight-asses you dated probably sounded different. Like a baby bird, begging for food or something."

Spencer smirked. "Meow, Pinky. I've never seen this side of you."

"Never dated a woman who farted before. Yeah, right. Like they didn't have rectums or something. Beautiful women with silicone boobs and no rectums. The perfect woman, according to Spencer Bolton."

I was on a roll and I couldn't stop. It might have been because of the humiliation of farting in front of my boyfriend, but it probably had more to do with the fact that I was Spencer's first farting girlfriend.

"Come here, farty girl," he said, grabbing for me.

"Oh please don't let that be my next nickname," I said and pushed him away. I pushed too hard and he was knocked off balance. He hit the wall behind him and then flung forward like he was a pinball game and I was the ball. He knocked me into the corner.

I fell flat on something. When I struggled to get back up, I understood what I had fallen on. I stood and debated with myself what to tell Spencer.

"It's not my fault," I said.

"What are you talking about?"

"Just remember that it's not my fault."

"Did you fart, again?"

"Nurse Millie might be dead in the corner of this closet," I said, like I was telling him that Grandma had moved the cans of baked beans to a new shelf in the kitchen.

I looked down at Millie. I didn't need to search for her pulse or listen for a heartbeat. No live person could get in her position. She was folded and rolled into the corner like someone wanted to stash her but also leave enough room for the bottles of disinfectant and the buckets and mops.

"Is that a joke?" Spencer asked. "Hey, I'm sorry about the fart comment. Everyone farts. I could fart right now. Do you want me to fart?"

I shook my head. "I don't want you to fart."

We stood for a moment, facing each other without saying a word.

"I'm waiting for you to say you're joking," Spencer

said.

"I know."

He walked around me and leaned over as much as he could in his body cast. He whistled long and slow. "She's dead, all right. She must have been killed right after you talked to her. Stabbed in the neck, it looks like."

"She was dead next to us while you were feeling me up," I pointed out.

Spencer ran a hand through his hair, as he studied the nurse's dead body. "What the hell is going on here? It doesn't add up. We need more information."

He was right. We needed more information. But even without more information, it was beginning to add up to me, like a jigsaw puzzle with just enough pieces to figure out the picture. My experience with Spencer, though, was that he didn't like my guessing and intuition when it came to murder. He liked to play by the book and I hadn't even read chapter one. So, I didn't tell him what I thought about Millie's murder and Mrs. Friendly's kidnapping.

Besides focusing on the mystery, my brain was giving me trouble in another area. It was playing havoc with my heart, which had a direct effect on my tear ducts. They filled up and spilled down my cheeks.

"She's dead because of me," I choked.

"No she's not."

I scowled at him. "Well, that didn't sound convincing."

"Well, she's sort of dead because of you. You're nosy as hell, Pinky. But she probably would have gotten stabbed in the neck, eventually. She was playing with bad guys. More than one. They were bound to kill her once the going got rough. They just didn't figure that you would get admitted to West Side and the going would get rough so soon."

I tried to make that out. "Thank you?"

He patted my shoulder. "No problem."

"It's not just that," I continued. "I think I'm becoming used to murdered people. I'm not really sad about her being stabbed in the neck."

"Well, to be fair, you've seen more murdered people than Jeffrey Dahmer."

"I'm Jeffrey Dahmer?"

"More like you're Jeffrey Dahmer adjacent," Spencer said, thoughtfully.

"I'm supposed to be in the love business."

"If only you could find a way to make money from finding dead people, you'd be rich. Come on. I have a plan."

Spencer's plan involved the hospital's two nighttime security guards, which brought the attention of Dr. Fric, who was worried that we were going to upset the patients again. After each of them inspected poor Nurse Millie, the doctor shut the closet door with a soft click and brought us to his office to discuss the matter away from the patients.

The doctor had a corner office with large windows that gave us a ring-side seat to the lightning storm outside. Every couple minutes, leaves and branches hit the windows. If *Psycho* was happening inside the hospital, *Twister* was happening outside.

I took a seat in a nubuck and chrome chair by the doctor's desk. He had fancy artwork on his walls, the modern art kind with only a couple squiggly lines and a splotch of paint here and there. I picked up a glass ball from his desk. Gently, Dr. Fric took the ball out of my hand and put it back on the desk.

"That's a Dale Chihuly," he said.

"Sorry."

The doctor sat in his large, leather chair and leaned back. Spencer and the security guards remained standing. The security guards were two older men who looked like deer caught in the headlights. Spencer seemed unhappy at the idea of taking orders from a doctor, but I would have bet money that he was only placating the doctor and would take control as soon as the doctor was done with the meeting.

"I think we all need to take a deep breath," the doctor started.

"How long will that take?" Spencer asked.

Dr. Fric's jaw worked like he was grinding his teeth, and he adjusted his position in his chair. "I understand that out in the world, you're a police officer."

"Chief of Police of Cannes," Spencer interrupted.

"I stand corrected. But we're outside of Cannes' boundaries, and you're out of commission, Mr. Bolton."

"Hey, I'm standing here, ready to go," Spencer growled. He was standing there in a hospital gown, no-slip footies, and a body cast with his arm stuck out at his side, as if he was looking for something to lean on. Even though he was a big, imposing man with a definite aura of authority, he wasn't at his most convincing.

"I'm just saying that maybe you sit this one out and let our able security team handle this."

Spencer ignored that suggestion. "Here's what we're going to do. Your able security team is going to go floor to floor to search for the attacker, who we can now call the murderer. There's a good chance he's still here because nobody is getting far in the storm. Meanwhile, you—Dr. Fric—will get the nurse down to the morgue and bring me the orderly."

"The orderly?"

"You remember the one. He said Mrs. Friendly didn't exist."

Dr. Fric furrowed his brow. "What does he have to do with this?"

Spencer hopped a couple times on his heels. "I'm betting my twelve years in law enforcement that he knows how to use a knife."

"Fine," Dr. Fric said after a moment. "About Mrs. Friendly, I'm afraid that you were entirely correct, Ms. Burger."

"I was?" I asked.

He nodded, the picture of regret. "Mrs. Friendly was your roommate for a matter of minutes. Then she had a major stroke and we moved her. For a moment, we mistook her identity, but it's worked out now."

"It's worked out?" I asked.

"I'm not strictly allowed to tell you this, but under the circumstances, I have to tell you that Mrs. Friendly passed away about an hour ago," he continued.

I could feel Spencer's eyes on me. He was probably waiting for me to freak out or have a Miss Marple moment, but my freakout, Miss Marple moment was hours away. I had other things to do before then.

"Thank you for your time," I said, like I was a calm and cool adult. "I'll go back to my room, now."

I stood up and effectively ended the meeting. Spencer barked orders at the security guards as we left the office, telling one to start on the roof and the other to start at the basement and to meet in the middle. I tapped him on the shoulder.

"What is it?" he asked me.

"Come with me."

"You want me to take you to your room?"

"Sure. Why not."

"Okay. You guys start," he told the guards. "I'll meet back up with you."

He took my hand, and we walked toward the elevator. "We'll get this worked out, Pinky. Don't worry about it. I know it seems scary now because it's the middle of the night and there's the storm of the century outside, but I've been through worse. By morning, I'll have this locked up."

I turned a little to the left.

"Where are we going?" he asked.

"Over there."

"Anyway, I've done this sort of thing a million times, Pinky," Spencer continued. "Did I ever tell you the time I captured a coke dealer in L.A.? I was trapped with his gang in a warehouse for three hours, but I came out on top."

"You never told me."

I held his hand while we walked behind the abandoned reception desk. I began to open all of the drawers.

"And there was one time in San Diego when…What are you doing?"

"I'm looking for a tool kit," I said, opening and closing the drawers.

"Oh. Why are you doing that?"

"Found it!" I announced, taking a box out of the bottom drawer. I opened it and pulled out a hammer. "Okay," I told Spencer, holding the hammer over my head. "Don't move. I have to aim this just right."

"Pinky, why are you aiming the hammer at me?"

"It shouldn't hurt too much."

CHAPTER 12

There comes a time in a relationship where the matches have to go all in or back out. There shouldn't be any hemming or hawing. A man will tell you that he likes the woman just a bissell, but she's nothing special. You tell him: Boychick, move on. But he's too nervous. Will he find someone else? Maybe she's the best around. No! Don't let your matches settle, dolly. These days, I'm seeing a lot of laziness in the settling business. It's hard for people to get off the couch, let alone to change direction in the love department. Tell them that this isn't low carb. It's not paleo. Ditto Weight Watchers. This is love. There are no cheat days.

Lesson 101, Matchmaking advice from your
Grandma Zelda

Spencer was terrified. It was more than his usual fear-of-commitment face. He was scared for his life. I sort of enjoyed making him scared, but we didn't have a lot of time for me to play with him.

"Stop being a baby," I said with the hammer over my head.

He took a step back. "Pinky, I'm sorry about the fart thing. I told you I'm sorry about the fart thing."

"Can you please shut up about the fart thing? I'd like to forget about the fart thing, if it's all the same to you."

"Forgotten. Now, put down the hammer."

"No."

"But I love you."

I lowered my arm. "I love you, too. That's why I'm going to break you out of your cast."

"Have you been sniffing glue?"

"Haven't you figured out what's going on here?" I asked.

"You mean your psychotic break?"

"All the pieces fit together," I said, ignoring his snarky comment. "I come in for a concussion and presto chango, I need my appendix out, but I feel fine. I mean, I feel fine after the farting incident that we won't talk about. And that man whose wife came in for heartburn? Now's she's going to have surgery, too. And then there's the glass balls."

Spencer jutted his neck out and squinted his eyes. "You're going to have to give me more than glass balls for me to follow your train of thought."

"Dr. Fric's office isn't the office of a country doctor. It's the office of a Goldman Sachs executive. Those balls are worth more than my grandmother's house. I can only imagine what kind of car he's got parked in his doctor parking spot."

"Go on," Spencer said.

"How does your arm feel?"

"Fine. Go on. Keep talking about your theory."

"This is part of it," I said, gesturing with the hammer. "Tell me how your arm feels."

"Fine. It feels fine."

I leaned forward until my face was almost touching his. "Spencer, your arm was broken in a bunch of places. You had a fist fight with a guy a couple of hours ago with your broken arm. Your arm should hurt like hell."

Spencer's mouth dropped open. "Look at you, Miss Marple," he breathed. "You impress the hell out of me."

I smiled. I liked impressing him. It made me feel all warm and melty inside. I raised the hammer, again. "That's not all. I'll tell you the rest after I break you out of your cast. Stand still."

He stepped back. "Wait a minute. Your theory has merit. You're probably right. But what if you're not?"

I scratched the side of my head with the hammer. "Then, I guess this will hurt like a bitch."

It turned out that it wasn't easy to break a body cast apart. I had figured it would be like a piñata, but West Side Hospital made a mean cast. I wacked the supporting pole a few times, and it came loose, freeing Spencer's arm from his body, but I couldn't get the rest off.

"You were right," Spencer said. "It doesn't hurt. We need new tools. Let's go to urgent care."

At urgent care, we found a power saw, but no matter how much I begged, Spencer wouldn't let me take a saw to his body. Instead, he shouted about his police chief status, and under protest, a nurse sawed him out of his cast.

Spencer moved his arm around in a big circle. "It's stiff and I've got a couple of nasty bruises, but it's fine," he said, giving me his I'm impressed smile, again. "Those sons of bitches. You think you've seen it all."

"They were going to operate on me tomorrow."

"I know," he said, wrapping his two arms around me and giving me a squeeze. "I'm going to do a lot of nasty stuff to you when this is all done," he whispered in my ear, making me shiver. "So tell me, Miss Marple, what happens next?"

"We're going to save Mrs. Friendly."

"But Mrs. Friendly is dead."

"Ha! Good one."

We entered the elevator, and I pushed the button. "Is this what it's normally like?" Spencer asked.

"What?"

"Your sleuthing."

"No. Normally I wear shoes while I do it."

"If the Mrs. Friendly thing doesn't pan out, we're doing the rest my way," he said.

I nodded, even though there was no way I was doing it his way. Still, sometimes it was good to choose the path of least resistance and let a man think he was in charge. Same with toddlers and flight attendants.

The elevator doors opened and we looked both ways before stepping out. "Shh," I told Spencer. He rolled his eyes.

Halfway down the hallway, I could see that Mrs. Friendly's door was open. As we got closer, I could hear voices from inside. We plastered ourselves against the wall and listened.

"This is way above my pay grade," one voice said.

"That's one of the security guards," Spencer whispered.

"Don't worry. You'll get paid enough. Just keep your mouth shut," another voice said from inside the room.

I shuffled along the wall and peeked inside the room, even though Spencer was making a bunch of signals for me not to. Inside the room, the security guard and the orderly were lifting the mummy-wrapped Mrs. Friendly off her bed and onto a stretcher. I ducked out, again.

"They're taking her," I whispered to Spencer. "Now's our chance."

"What do you mean?" he hissed back.

"Just follow my lead."

"But…"

I walked into the hospital room, like I was out for a stroll in Hyde Park. "What are you doing here?" the orderly demanded. He was obviously surprised to see me, but not as much as the security guard, who definitely had a hand-in-the-cookie-jar look.

"We," I started and looked behind me, but Spencer hadn't come into the room. "I mean, I needed some water. Do you have any water?" I could have sworn I heard Spencer say *Are you kidding me?* from the hall.

"Go back to your room and hit your call button. Someone will come to give you water," the orderly said.

I snuck a glance at Mrs. Friendly and tried to make out if she was breathing or not. It was hard to tell in the wrapping. They must have seen me looking because they draped a sheet over her.

"You have to leave now, ma'am. We have to take this patient to the morgue."

"Oh, okay," I said, smiling. Then, I clutched my chest and rolled my eyes back in my head. "My heart! My heart! It's happening!"

"What's happening?" the security guard shrieked.

"Help me, lord! My heart!"

I spun around, flailing my arms. I wasn't totally sure what I was doing, but I knew that I couldn't let them take Mrs. Friendly. Once she was out of sight, who knew what would happen to her. Already, they were telling the world that she was dead, so there was a pretty good chance that she would wind up that way for real.

I slapped my forehead with the back of my hand. "The world is spinning!" I threw myself on the bed and shut my eyes. Yes, it was melodramatic. Yes, I had no chance of it working, but I didn't know what else to do. Even with Spencer, I didn't think we could strong arm two bad guys. The security guard had mace and the orderly had access to heavy-duty pharmaceuticals. So, I took a shot.

"Is she dead?" the security guard asked the orderly.

"Don't be a moron."

"You better get someone."

There was a long pause while I held my breath.

"Fine. I'll be right back. Don't move a muscle. Don't let the old broad get away."

I assumed that I wasn't the old broad he was talking about. I opened one eye, just as Spencer burst into the room. "Give me the old broad and I won't break your face," he growled at the security guard. The guard lifted his hands in surrender.

I got up from the bed and grabbed onto the stretcher like I was wheeling a cart at the grocery store. "What are you doing?" Spencer asked.

"Hurry before he comes back. The conspiracy is large. We have to get her out of here."

I pushed Mrs. Friendly, making a beeline for the door.

"You never saw us!" Spencer yelled at the security guard and followed me out. He took hold of the stretcher and we ran for the elevator. "I have no idea where we're going."

"Outta here. Hurry up."

When we got to the elevator, I pushed the call button. A second later, the doors opened. The orderly was inside "I knew it!" he yelled, pointing at me.

"You didn't get help? I could have died."

"Now's not the time," Spencer told me, running back the way we came with the stretcher. "I'm sensing a flaw in your plan, Pinky."

As we ran past the hospital rooms, a door flew open, and Lucy stepped out. "What on earth?" she asked.

"Help! We need back up!" I yelled.

She looked from Spencer and me with our stretcher to the orderly who was closing in fast. "Cletus!" she called. "The Hatfield boys got the still!"

I heard an inhuman cry and I turned my head while I ran with Spencer. Cletus had run out of his room and tackled the orderly to the ground behind us.

"Go, Gladie!" Lucy called.

We ran around the corner past the nurses' desk and two nurses with their mouths open, then around another corner until we got to what looked like a freight elevator. I pushed the call button and when it arrived, we took it to the bottom floor.

"My kingdom for my gun," Spencer said, as we waited for the elevator to arrive. "I've never run away before. Normally, I'm the chaser, not the chased."

"After we get Mrs. Friendly out of here, you can put everyone in prison," I said to make him happy.

But when the doors opened at the bottom floor, the orderly and the two security guards were waiting for us. They looked madder than spit. The guards held mace and the orderly was pounding his fist into his other hand.

"I'm the chief of police," Spencer said, but they didn't

seem to care.

"We don't care," the orderly said.

Spencer took a step forward out of the elevator and smiled. "Let me help you guys," he said. "You're in over your heads, here. California still has the death penalty, you know. You don't want to end up that way."

"We're not going to end up that way," one of the guards said. "You are."

"I don't think you understand the gravity of killing a cop. There will be a tidal wave of shit on your heads. You don't want that," Spencer continued, getting nowhere as far as I could tell.

Spencer's back was to me, and his arms were out, as if he were trying to shield me. I was still in the elevator. Mrs. Friendly's stretcher was half in and half out, triggering the elevator doors to re-open each time they tried to close. I made sure that she was belted in tight, because I knew she was going to be in for a rough ride.

Because I knew what I had to do.

Well, I didn't really know what I had to do, but I figured anything was better than waiting to be killed by three thugs. Spencer was being brave, but from my vantage point, he was just a tall, good-looking guy with his butt sticking out of his hospital gown.

I stepped behind the stretcher and wrapped my hands around its handles. I took a deep breath to prepare myself for what I was about to do. I silently chastised myself for not being in shape and made a promise to the universe to go to the gym if I survived.

"All right guys, if that's the way you want to play this," Spencer was saying, putting up his fists, like he was going to box them all. "If I had a gun I would have shot all of you by now, but beating you senseless will have to do for now."

I focused on my plan. I bent my knees and pulled the stretcher back and then in a burst of energy, pushed forward, running full out. "Outta my way!" I shouted. I rammed the stretcher between the men.

I heard the sound of mace being sprayed, but they were behind me and the mace couldn't get near my eyes. I ran through the lobby with them on my heels. There was the occasional *oomph!* and *argh!* and I figured that Spencer was doing his best to be my backup. I ran to the integrative medicine room and opened the door. It was difficult to push the stretcher in while holding the door open, which gave my pursuers time to make up ground. Spencer was holding back the guards, but the orderly reached me and grabbed hold of my scrubs just as I got the stretcher into the room.

I tried to run, but he held me back. "Let me go!" I

yelled and gave him the perfect knee to his balls. It was just like in the movies. I made direct contact, and he sucked in air, doubling over for just long enough for me to run into the room. I closed the door behind me and searched for a lock, but there wasn't one. No way to bar the door, either.

"Sonofabitch," I moaned.

I grabbed hold of the stretcher again and looked around. The room was empty, but the coals were still there. They weren't glowing anymore, but as I approached, I could feel the heat coming off them. I ran the stretcher around to the other side of the strip of coals, just as the door opened and the orderly ran inside.

Panicked, I looked around for a door or a window, any kind of exit, but I had literally put myself into a corner. The orderly walked slowly into the room, stopping on the other side of the coals. "No place to run," he said, smiling. "This is going to be fun."

I didn't know what he meant by that and I didn't want to find out. I tried to think about what James Bond or Wonder Woman would do, but I didn't have a weapon or a lasso. I just had me and that wasn't a match for a mean orderly. I was going to die, murdered and stuffed in a closet or wrapped like a mummy and sent off to die somewhere where no one would help me.

I closed my eyes and hoped for a miracle.

"Get off me!" I heard and opened my eyes.

Spencer was being manhandled, dragged in by the two security guards. His eyes were red, probably from being maced, but the guards were the ones who looked worse for wear. One had a bloody, broken nose and the other one had a doozy of a black eye.

Spencer stopped struggling when he saw me facing off with the orderly. His face changed into something terrifying. Focused.

He yanked the guard with the broken nose closer, shrugged out of his grasp and punched him square in the nose, again, smashing it into a pancake and making it spray blood. The guard dropped to his knees and clutched his face in agony. Spencer spun around and punched the other guard, but he sprayed Spencer in the face, blinding him.

"You should have picked a better hero," the orderly sneered at me. He took a step to the right, starting to walk around the coals toward me and Mrs. Friendly.

I shook with fear. Things were not going well, and I had run out of miracles.

"Nobody touches my still!"

Lucy's brother Cletus burst through the door, his hospital gown flying upward. The last I saw of him, he was going crazy on the orderly upstairs, but the orderly must have gotten the better of him. Now Cletus was back for a second round.

Cletus was my miracle.

He ran in and clotheslined the standing guard with his arm outstretched, catching the guard under his neck. The guard went down and Cletus kept coming. Spencer wiped his eyes and followed.

"I hate you the most," Cletus announced and knocked the orderly with his shoulder, like he was Mean Joe Greene at the five-yard line. The orderly sailed through the air and waved his arms, as if he was trying to fly.

But the orderly couldn't fly. He fell down and landed splat on the hot coals.

The good die young and no good deed goes unpunished. But sometimes when karma doesn't do its job, a guy named Cletus comes along and does it.

The orderly landed on his hands and knees and screamed. Spencer leaped over the coals to me. "Are you okay?" he asked me.

"Let's get the hell out of here," I said, pushing the stretcher. I ran it around the coals and didn't look back.

"How about you, man?" Spencer asked Cletus, as we ran by. He looked down at the men he had attacked. They were all getting up, and the orderly pulled a gun out of his scrubs with a shaky hand.

"I'll be right in front of you!" Cletus yelled and ran out of the room.

Spencer helped me push the stretcher, as we ran for our lives because men can be macho, but they can't be bulletproof. As we got through the door, the first shot rang out. Spencer pushed me in between him and the stretcher to shield me and we followed Cletus out. We didn't stop running until we got outside into the storm.

"This is worse than bullets!" I shouted against the wind and rain.

It really was the storm of the century. Trees were down, the sky was bright with lightning, and the wind was gale force. I was soaked through almost immediately.

"What?" Spencer shouted back.

"This is really bad!"

"What!"

We were getting nowhere. Literally. But if we didn't get somewhere, we were going to die along with Mrs. Friendly.

"No way out!" Cletus shouted.

"What!" Spencer shouted back.

"There!" I shouted. The lights of an ambulance were barely visibly through the storm. I pushed the stretcher, and Spencer and Cletus followed me. "Put her in back," I told Cletus.

He opened the back door, and I went around to the front and tried the door. "What are you doing?" a paramedic asked, coming out of the storm with an umbrella.

"They need you inside!" I told him. "Hurry! It's an emergency!"

He believed me and ran back into the hospital. I opened the driver's door. "The keys are in it," I told Spencer. "You drive and I'll stay in back with Mrs. Friendly."

"Be careful."

"Aren't I always?"

I ran to the back of the ambulance, as Spencer started it up. "He's in!" Cletus said. "Too crowded in there. I'm going to take my chances getting back to town on my own."

"What? Are you crazy? In this weather?"

"This is nothing. Besides, I have my eye on a doctor's Jaguar. Won't take much to hot wire it. Uh oh. Here they come!"

The orderly and his henchmen had spotted us. I climbed in the back and shut the doors. I pounded on the window between me and Spencer. "Hurry! They're coming!"

Spencer put the car into gear and took off into the storm.

"Not again," I heard someone say.

At first, I thought it was Mrs. Friendly, but it was a man's voice. That's when I realized that we weren't alone. The man with the arrow in his head was lying on a second stretcher next to Mrs. Friendly.

"Uh," I said.

He looked up at me with fearful eyes. "I don't understand what's happening."

That was the understatement of the year.

CHAPTER 13

Alpha. That's what it's called when a man's grumpy, right, dolly? No, not grumpy...what's it called? Oh, yes. MANLY. Manly men are alphas. That's what women want right now. Those are the Navy Seal, firefighter, cowboy types. They have washboard abs and a limited vocabulary. Alpha men are great in a crisis, if the crisis doesn't involve washing the dishes or picking up the kids from school. So, if your lady matches want help with dishes or picking up the kids, match them with a nice, easygoing Beta. But if they're looking for a non-talking, he-man, wonderboy, then go Alpha all the way, bubeleh. Where can you find these Alphas? Check their abs. Their abs are a dead giveaway.

Lesson 36, Matchmaking advice from your Grandma Zelda

When I was fourteen, I decided I needed my own money, so I got a job cleaning pots and pans at the diner on the corner. I was paid three dollars an hour in cash and all of the day-old pie I could eat. I was treated like family and I thought I was the richest girl in the world. It was my first job and I would have done it for years, but one day there was a storm, and a lightning strike hit a nearby electrical pole. The pole split in two, and the electrical wire went wild, whipping around until it landed on the diner's wooden roof shingles. I saw it all because it happened five minutes before I was due to start. I stood in the parking lot while I watched the lightning, the pole, and the wild wire. It all happened within a matter of seconds. The wood shingles went up in a fireball. Luckily, the diners and the workers got out before the building was incinerated. With the diner gone, I turned around and got another job. I worked at the local arcade for three days until I got stuck in a claw machine, and it took the local firefighters an hour and a half and twenty-five dollars to get me out.

I totally blamed the lightning.

"Are you transferring me to the other hospital?" the man with the arrow in his head asked me. "They were taking me there to…well…get away from you."

"Sure, why not? We'll take you to the other hospital,"

I said.

The ambulance bumped and swerved over the debris in the road, which had been blown there by the storm. Arrow gasped.

"I'm sure it'll be fine," I lied. Spencer was driving like a madman through the storm of the century. The ambulance was tough, but I didn't think it could survive this.

"I'm not supposed to be jostled," the man with the arrow in his head said.

I opened the window between us and the front seat. "Spencer, can you slow it down? We have a guest back here."

"What? What guest?" He looked behind him and the ambulance swerved violently. I lost my balance and fell onto Mrs. Friendly's stretcher.

"I'm getting jostled," Arrow said. "I'm not supposed to get jostled. They distinctly told me, no jostling."

"Who's that?" Spencer asked, righting the ambulance.

"It's Arrow. I mean, Mr. Hood. He was being transferred to another hospital because…well, because of me."

Spencer shook his head. "Yep. I'm in the Gladie vortex all right."

"You're going to have to slow it down," I said,

ignoring the vortex comment.

"I would, but we're being followed."

"By the hospital goons?"

"Yes," Spencer said. "Them and a tornado."

I didn't tell Arrow about the tornado. Tornadoes were infamous for jostling.

"Ohhh." There was a woman moaning. At first, I thought it was me, but it was coming from Mrs. Friendly. I held onto her stretcher for support while I made my way to her. I leaned over her face.

"Mrs. Friendly?

"Ohhh…"

She was alive. It had been a long struggle to get to speak to her again. I was so relieved that she was still breathing and speaking, even if it was only a moan. "Mrs. Friendly? Oh, Mrs. Friendly. I'm so glad you're okay."

"Who the hell is Mrs. Friendly? What's on my face?" she asked, her mouth muffled by the bandages.

She tried to remove the wrappings, but her arms were strapped down. I released her arms and helped her to unwrap her face. There she was. Mrs. Friendly. Her glasses were gone, and her hair was a mess, but it was the woman I had remembered from my hospital room.

"What happened? Where am I?" she asked.

"You're in an ambulance. We stole it to save you."

"I thought you were transferring me," the man with the arrow in his head said.

"What's that in his head?" Mrs. Friendly asked me.

"It's an arrow," he replied. "It's the darndest story how it got there."

"I don't care how it got there," she said. "We need to find the police."

I pointed at Spencer. "He's already here."

"Good. We need to arrest everyone at the hospital. Clean up the whole damned place."

She was right, except about the "we" part. I was all for fleeing the scene and having Spencer's men arrest everyone while I was far away. In my bed, preferably.

"They're gaining on us!" Spencer shouted. The ambulance groaned as Spencer accelerated, pushing the vehicle to its limits.

"Who's gaining on us?" I asked. "The bad guys or the tornado?"

"Tornado?" Mrs. Friendly asked.

"I'm never going to an archery field again," the man with the arrow in his head said.

"I wish the damned communication system would work!" Spencer yelled.

It didn't look good. Everyone was freaking out at the same time, and the ambulance was having a hard time with the wet mountain roads and the gusty winds. Spencer was a good driver, but he was up against a pissed off Mother Nature and three bad guys with a better car. If we were going to die or worse, I wanted to at least get the real story behind Mrs. Friendly's disappearance.

"What happened to you?" I asked. "I searched for you all over the hospital. They said you didn't exist and then they told me you were dead."

She worked on her wrappings and I helped her to sit up. I sat next to her on the stretcher. "I sort of didn't exist. That's true. I'm not really Mrs. Friendly," she said.

"You're not?"

"My name's Frieda Wilson. I'm a P.I."

"You're a P.I.?" the man with the arrow in his head asked her.

"I was hired to investigate the hospital," she continued.

"Because of the false diagnoses to drum up income, right?" I asked.

She shot me a look of surprise. "You figured that out in a matter of hours? I'm impressed."

I felt my face get hot with embarrassment. "I'm sort of nosy."

"Good for you. Anyway, I got too close. The damned orderly or the bitch nurse must have drugged me. The next thing I knew, I was waking up here."

I filled her in on what I knew and about the nurse's murder. She told me that the ringleader was the orderly, so he probably killed the nurse and attacked me and Spencer. That's what we had figured, too, but the conspiracy couldn't have begun and ended with just them.

"Who hired you?" I asked.

"A rich man who went in to remove a mole and came out with an unnecessary pacemaker."

I thought back to the old man with the pacemaker and wondered if he really needed his. There would have to be a complete audit of the hospital and a review of all of its patients if we ever got out of this alive.

"It's blowing like a sonofabitch!" Spencer yelled. "Hold on to your hats."

"I resent that comment," Arrow said.

"They're coming up from behind us," Spencer warned. "Here we go!"

The ambulance made a sharp turn to the left, crashed into the car that was chasing us, and righted itself. Mrs. Friendly and I grabbed onto each other for support.

"They're still coming!" Spencer yelled.

The ambulance was bumped from behind, and we skidded into the shoulder for a moment, but Spencer got it back on the road quickly. Spencer cheered. "They ran off the road," he announced. "We're home free!"

"You did it!" I cheered.

"We're in the clear now. We'll be back home in thirty minutes."

"What's that noise?" the man with the arrow in his head asked. "Oh, no. I was jostled, and now I'm hearing things."

"I hear it, too," I told him. "It sounds like…"

Like doom.

Like a horrible death.

Like a tornado.

"I haven't heard that sound since I lived in Oklahoma," Mrs. Friendly said.

We held onto each other for dear life.

"A cow just flew by!" Spencer announced. "There's another one! And there's...Whoa!"

Whoa was right. The ambulance rose in the air and began to spin around.

Everyone screamed. It was like the Beatles at Shea Stadium.

We spun and spun. It went on for so long that I was sure we were going to die. But we didn't. Finally, the noise died down, and the ambulance fell from the air and landed with a thud. The inside of the ambulance was a mess, but the stretchers were locked down and hadn't moved. Arrow had stayed in his place, but Mrs. Friendly and I had to hold on to her stretcher so we wouldn't hit our heads on the ceiling when the ambulance fell.

"We're okay. We're okay," Spencer announced. "A tree broke our fall."

"I'm going to be sick," I said. I had never been very

good with rollercoasters and spinning rides at amusement parks. I hopped off the stretcher and threw up in the corner of the ambulance. Mrs. Friendly kindly held my hair while I tossed my cookies.

"You have lovely hair, my dear," she said while I retched.

"Thank you," I said after I finished. "I've been using a new conditioner."

The back doors opened and Spencer looked in. The storm had died down to a gentle rain. We were in the middle of a field, high up in the mountains. Wildlife was making a lot of sounds, as if the animals were talking among themselves to make sure they had made it out of the tornado alive. Spencer's hospital gown was soaked through, and he had a gash on his forehead. I checked myself for injuries. Miraculously, I was fine. So was Mrs. Friendly.

There was no sound coming from Arrow, and I dreaded checking on him, because I was sure of his fate. There was no way being thrown around in a tornado wasn't considered big-time jostling.

I crawled to his stretcher. "Arrow? I mean, Mr. Hood?" I asked. I crouched by his stretcher and watched for his breathing. His chest moved up and down, and his eyes were open. So, he was alive. "Can you speak in full sentences?" I asked him.

He lifted his hand up. In it, he was holding his arrow.

"Oh my God," I said.

Arrow unstrapped himself and sat up. "The arrow fell out," he said. "Plop. Out."

I studied his head where the arrow was. "It's not even bleeding."

"I know. Crazy, right?"

"It's like your brain pushed it out," Mrs. Friendly said.

"Those doctors were wrong," he said. "Jostling cured me!"

There was a general feeling of euphoria in the ambulance, which came from the unbelievable fact that we had all survived being tossed in a tornado and chased by murderous thugs. The rain stopped and the sun began to rise, the serene sign of second chances. Suddenly, everything else seemed doable and easy, like a conspiracy in a hospital wasn't such a big deal and it could be handled easily in the light of a beautiful day.

"Okay, everybody," Spencer said. "I think the ambulance made it out fine. So, how about we drive into town and out of this nightmare?"

"Sounds good to me!" Arrow said, happy as a clam.

"I have a report to file," Mrs. Friendly said.

"That's why we're going to the precinct. We're going to get this thing worked out."

I took a deep breath and relaxed for the first time since the night before. I wanted to make sure that Lucy was all right and get her out of West Side Hospital, but I was sure that Spencer would act quickly.

"I'm ready to go," I said, giving Spencer my biggest smile. My hero. He had managed to get us to safety against all odds.

Spencer began to close the doors when there was a loud popping sound.

"Somebody popping corn?" Arrow asked.

"Duck!" Spencer shouted. "Shots fired!"

There was another pop. Spencer yelped in pain and dropped to the ground. "I'm not sticking around," Mrs. Friendly announced as she jumped out of the ambulance and began to run across the field. Once again, an old lady was in better shape than I was.

"Your friend got shot," Arrow told me, as he tried to hide under a stretcher.

"Spencer!" I yelled and went to check on him. The side of his head was bleeding, and he was out cold.

"Bullets are worse than arrows," Arrow pointed out.

I shook Spencer, trying to revive him. "Spencer, please don't die," I pleaded. Then, I felt a searing pain at the back of my head and everything went black.

CHAPTER 14

This business sees a lot of tears. Some theirs. Some ours. Mostly theirs, though. That's because love comes with tsuris, bubeleh. Piles of tsuris. Yes, we're problem-solvers. But the heart isn't a problem. It is what it is. It feels what it feels. When it's broken, it takes time to heal. So, a good part of our job is to put an arm around a match and give them a big helping of tea and sympathy. In the end, the heart heals itself, though. We're just there to make the healing process easier. Kinder.

Lesson 73, Matchmaking advice from your
Grandma Zelda

I was unconscious, but I could see a bright light.

Uh oh.

So, this is how it ends, I thought. Surviving a tornado,

gunshots, and fake appendicitis to die like this.

Like how? How was I dying?

I had no idea. All I knew was that I was unconscious and there was a bright light. Where was God? Where was my father? Oh, no. Maybe my bright light was directing me in the wrong direction. Maybe Hitler and Pol Pot were going to show up and drag me to my room in hell.

Dying sucks.

The light got brighter, but now I wanted no part of it. I didn't want a room in hell. I didn't want to be best buds with Hitler. I swatted at the bright light with my hands, but my hands couldn't reach it. I had very short hands. What was wrong with my hands? My hands were…tied down.

Suddenly, I regained consciousness and I opened my eyes.

My hands were strapped down to an operating table and there was a bright light in my face. An operating room bright light.

I looked around. To my left was a table of medical tools. To my right was another operating table and Spencer was lying unconscious on it.

I closed my eyes again and willed myself to be dead on my way to hell.

I counted to ten and opened my eyes again.

Nope. I was still in the operating room.

A door opened and Dr. Fric walked in. "Awake?" he asked me.

"No," I croaked. "I'm pretty sure I'm having a bad dream."

He leaned over me, putting his head between me and the light. He was a good-looking man, despite his goatee and the fact that he had kidnapped me.

"Don't worry," he said. "This bad dream won't last long. Your surgery is about to start and then you won't have long left."

I fought a rising tide of hysteria. I had woken to all of my worst fears wrapped up into one hellish scene. I swallowed. "Don't you want to know my list of allergies? I thought they asked that before an operation."

"Not this kind of operation."

He's seemed very pleased with this line of discussion. I wanted to punch him in the face.

"Doesn't sound very professional to me. Like maybe you're not a real doctor," I said, keeping my voice accusatory, not hysterical.

His smile dropped into a scowl. "I'm a real doctor."

"A real doctor would ask about my allergies."

"I'm a real doctor."

I shrugged my shoulders. "If you say so, but…"

"All right. Just to make you happy since you have precious few seconds left on this earth, what are you allergic to?"

"Surgery."

He squinted at me, as if he was trying to understand. No sense of humor…the worst kind of doctor. He shook his head and walked to a side table, where he gathered some tools.

I looked to my right. Spencer was still out cold. "Did you operate on Spencer?" I asked, fighting my lip, which wanted to quiver.

"He's after you. He's going to die of his injuries."

My eyes threatened to fill up with tears, but I refused to let myself cry. "He has injuries?"

"Actually, he was only grazed. Shot in the head, and he only needs a Band-Aid. Amazing, right?"

I exhaled and breathed easy for a second. At least

Spencer was all right. I just had to get him out of there before the doctor killed him.

Dr. Fric set up an IV next to me. "Why are you doing this?" I asked. "Why are you working for the orderly? Be a hero. If you rat him out, I'm sure the police will cut you a deal."

"You think I work for that guy? The guy with the sixth-grade education?"

Dumb Gladie. Dumb, dumb, dumb Gladie. Of course he wasn't working for the orderly. It had to be the other way around. The doctor had pretended to be nice, as if he had gotten an A in his bedside manner class, but actually, he was a scheming, sadistic criminal.

Duh.

"I figured out that you were pulling a scam," I said. "Misdiagnosing patients so you could buy glass balls."

"And a vacation home in the south of France. And a Saville Row wardrobe. And a home theater system that would knock your socks off."

"But you went further," I said. "When you realized that Mrs. Friendly was really a private detective, you plotted to get rid of her."

He tied a strip of rubber around my upper arm and

searched for a vein. "It was just like an episode of Scooby Doo," he said. "I would have gotten away with it if it wasn't for you meddling kids. We were going to transfer her in the morning and have her die in transit, far away from me. But you refused to leave it alone. 'Where's Mrs. Friendly? Where's Mrs. Friendly?' You were like a dog with a bone."

"And Nurse Millie grew a conscience."

Dr. Fric found my vein and pushed in the needle. "That bitch had made more money because of me than she would have in ten years as a nurse. Let me tell you something. There's no loyalty in the workplace anymore. I don't know what kind of world we're living in. Everything's gone to hell."

I nodded, agreeing with him.

He attached the IV tube to the needle in my arm. "So, do you want to know what I'm going to do to you?"

"Probably not." I so didn't want to know. I wanted to know how much I weighed more than I wanted to know what he was going to do to me. I wanted to know the details of my iTunes contract more than I wanted to know what he was going to do to me.

I was about to pass out from fear. There were knives in the room and other tools that I didn't know people used on other people. The smell was disinfectant and sadism instead of disinfectant and caring. Doctors were supposed to be caring and kind. They weren't supposed to torture and kill their patients.

Dr. Fric sucked ass as a doctor.

"Lobotomy."

"Excuse me?" I asked, startled.

He leaned down and whispered in my ear. "I've never done one, but I've always wanted to."

"But…"

"After that, your appendix is going to burst." He used air quotes when he said, 'burst.' "I didn't get to you in time because you were out stealing an ambulance. That's what the official report will be. It'll be an expensive report, but I'm willing to shell out the money for it."

"When you say lobotomy, you don't mean lobotomy, right? We're probably thinking about two different things." I said.

"Lobotomy. Lo-bot-o-my. Say bye-bye to your prefrontal cortex." He pulled a wood-handled tool off a table and showed it to me. "Ice pick," he said, proud of himself. "Just like the good old days."

"I need to go to the bathroom," I stammered.

Dr. Fric shook his head. "You'll have plenty of time

for that when you're dead."

Dead. Ice pick. I closed my eyes and willed myself to think a way out of this nightmare. Why wasn't I smarter? Why didn't I read more? People Magazine hadn't prepared me at all for this sort of situation. Who cared if Sandra Bullock had re-decorated her weight room? What did it matter if Chris Pratt had adopted a llama? Those facts didn't do a damned thing for me when I was strapped to an operating table with a maniacal doctor preparing to ice pick my brain.

What would Miss Marple do? Who was I kidding? Miss Marple would never have gotten into this mess. She would have solved the mystery long before she stole an ambulance and flew through the air in a tornado. By now, the bad guy would be in jail and Miss Marple would be knitting a new cardigan.

Grandma had been wrong. Not only did I not have the gift for love, I didn't have the gift for murder either. I was nothing more than a clumsy victim. My nosiness and incompetence had gotten me into this predicament and not only was I going to suffer, but Spencer was going to suffer along with me. And what had happened to Mrs. Friendly and Arrow? Were they even alive?

I deserved to be lobotomized with an ice pick.

But I didn't want to be lobotomized. I didn't want to

be terrorized. I didn't want to be murdered, and I didn't want Spencer or anyone else to suffer because of me. I could feel sorry for myself and berate myself later. Now was the time for action. I needed to escape and save Spencer. I needed to make things happen.

I was woman and I was about to roar. At least I was planning to roar.

But someone else roared before I got a chance.

There was a loud noise above us and things in the operating room clanged to the floor. It sounded like a bomb had gone off on the floor above us. "What the hell was that?" Dr. Fric demanded. He looked up, as if he expected something to crash through the ceiling, but nothing did, and there wasn't another loud noise. "It looks like no one is coming to your rescue, Ms. Burger. You ready?"

I wasn't ready. I was nowhere close to being ready.

The door to the operating room burst open, and one of the security guards ran in. He was still wet from the rain and his clothes were torn. "Come quick!" he yelled. "It's horrible! You gotta come! The lobby's destroyed!"

"What?" Dr. Fric asked, holding the ice pick.

"Now! Before it's too late!"

Dr. Fric looked at me and the ice pick and then at the

security guard. He sighed and walked out of the room. The minute the door closed behind him, I tried to wake Spencer.

"Psst! Psst! Spencer, wake up!"

But he was out cold. He wasn't only sleeping; he must have been given something that knocked him out.

So, it was up to me. It was time for me to roar.

I yanked at my bindings, but they wouldn't budge. However, my legs were free. I threw them off the table, and they landed on the floor with a thud, jamming my foot against one of the table wheels. I was still wearing the no-slip footies and the scrubs, which were still wet from the rain. I guessed Dr. Fric didn't need me to wear a special surgical gown to get lobotomized and murdered.

I unlocked the wheels of the table and rammed the table into the wall with all of my strength. I crashed it three times before one of my bindings came loose from the table. I unhooked my other hand and took out my IV. I ran to Spencer. He was breathing, but he wouldn't rouse, even after I slapped him.

I wheeled his table out of the operating room and pushed it quickly down the hallway. As I turned the corner, I heard Dr. Fric coming back with the orderly. They were arguing, but I didn't stop to listen to what they were saying. I had to hide with Spencer before they found us.

"It would be a lot easier if you woke up," I complained to the unconscious Spencer. I opened a door to the stairway. I couldn't wheel him upstairs, so I was going to have to carry him.

But I couldn't lift him. Once again, I was reminded of my lack of fitness. I rolled Spencer off the table and let his body land while I protected his head. Then, it was a matter of lifting him in pieces. One leg, another leg, and so on. By the time we got halfway up the first flight, I thought I was going to die. I couldn't breathe and my heart felt like it was going to explode.

"For a man with ten percent body fat, you sure are heavy," I complained, trying to catch my breath.

"Five percent," Spencer said.

"Spencer? Are you awake?"

"Holy shit, my head. What happened? Where am I? Am I still in the Gladie vortex?"

I covered his face in kisses. Relieved that he was alive and his normal self—and that I didn't have to carry him anymore—I couldn't restrain myself. I kissed every inch of his face and then told him everything.

"An ice pick," I told him. "He was going to stick it in my brain."

Spencer smirked.

"Don't you dare," I said.

"What?"

"You know what. You were going to say something about my brain and how I might be better off with some ice pick action."

Spencer kept smirking. "Hey, you said it, Pinky. Not me." He stood up, and gave me his hand. "I bet the phones are working now. I'm going to have Remington come in with the troops and finish this up. I'll tell him to bring my really big gun."

His smirk turned into a smile and, holding my hand, we climbed up the rest of the way to the first floor of the hospital.

"We need to find the doctor," I said.

"Fine. As soon as I have my really big gun."

We opened the door to the lobby and stopped in our tracks. All hell had broken loose. It was now about seven in the morning, and the sun was shining through the gaping hole in the wall where the front door used to be. The reception desk had been pulverized, and in its place was our stolen ambulance.

Next to the ambulance, Mrs. Friendly was sitting on a prone, unconscious security guard. "The police will be right here!" she yelled.

I turned to Spencer. "Looks like someone beat you to it. Maybe if you call, you can catch Remington before he leaves and ask him for your really big gun."

"He's probably already on his way. Damn it."

"I'm sure Grandma will let you shoot cans in her backyard."

"It's not the same," Spencer said, thoroughly disappointed.

"Gladie! Gladie!" Lucy floated toward us in her peach peignoir, stepping gingerly over the bits of building that the ambulance had destroyed. She waved at me, like she was a princess greeting her subjects.

"I knew you'd be around here somewhere," she said, reaching us. "I heard that an ambulance crashed through the front door and I said to myself, well that has to be Gladie."

"I wasn't driving," I said. "I was downstairs after the doctor kidnapped us. He tried to lobotomize me."

Lucy frowned. "Darn it. I miss everything."

"Stay with Lucy," Spencer told me. "I'm going to

make some calls."

"He sure is rockin' that hospital gown," Lucy said, as we watched him walk away with his butt in full view.

We sighed in unison.

"This hospital visit has revived me, Gladie," Lucy said. "I feel ready to get married now. This near-death experience has given me a new perspective. Love has nothing to do with hair or cake or if my wedding ring has been keeping my brother's penis company."

I hugged her and didn't point out that she hadn't actually had a near-death experience. I had cornered the market on those.

"Arrow!" I said, clutching Lucy's arm. "I forgot about him. I need to make sure he's all right."

"Who's Arrow?"

The police arrived. The entire Cannes police force invaded, like they were the cast of a war movie with Remington leading the platoon. He was hot and huge, and he was Spencer's only competent cop. I knew the whole force-- and I knew Remington biblically-- and a few of them gave me a nod when they came in with guns blazing.

"The cavalry's arrived," Lucy cheered, clapping her hands. "This is better than rodeo week in Flagstaff."

The police weren't alone. A big section of Cannes came with them to see what all the hubbub was about. Uncle Harry was among them, and I was surprised to see tears in the eyes of the tough guy when he found Lucy and gave her a kiss.

"I heard horrible things," he told her. "I thought I lost you."

"Oh, darlin', you could never lose me."

They started kissing with tongue, and I decided to give them some privacy. A minute later, Spencer and Remington came out with the orderly and the two security guards in handcuffs, but there was no sign of Dr. Fric.

I needed to remind Spencer about Arrow. I went outside where they were putting the bad guys into the paddy wagon. Remington was handing Spencer a really big gun, and Spencer was checking it.

"I thought you'd like to have it, boss," Remington said. "Oh, hello Gladie. You're looking beautimus. Cool uniform."

"Don't you have work to do?" Spencer growled at Remington. Spencer tried to be nonchalant about the fact that I had done the dirty deed with Remington before we were together, but usually Spencer wound up being plenty chalant.

Remington winked at me and got busy elsewhere. I reminded Spencer that Arrow and the doctor were still missing.

"Okay, Pinky. Leave the police work to the police, will you?"

"But…"

"Don't worry about anything. I'll handle it. Do you understand me?"

I cocked my head to the side. "Not really."

He patted my head. "I'm going to help out. You stay here. Do you hear me?"

"Are you patronizing me?" I asked.

"Yes. Stay here. Did you hear me?"

I nodded. "Stay here."

I was bone tired and I kind of liked feeling safe. I also kind of liked that Spencer was in charge with his really big gun and that he would take care of everything. Yes, I was worried about Arrow, especially since his abduction was entirely my fault. But with the whole police force looking for him, I felt I could finally relax.

"So, you stay here where you'll be safe," Spencer said.

"I'm going to stay here where I'll be safe," I echoed.

"Good girl," he said and went to help out with his really big gun.

I sat on the bumper of the paddy wagon and took stock. West Side Hospital was a mess. Nurse Millie had been murdered. But if Arrow was found okay, that meant that everyone else had made it out no worse for wear. In fact, my appendix was fine and so was Spencer's arm. So, we were better now than when we had been admitted.

"Not too bad for a day's work," I said, feeling happy with myself.

Then, I felt something sharp at my temple. "Don't try anything and don't say anything. You're coming with me."

I would have known that voice anywhere. It was my nemesis, and he had his ice pick at my head. He grabbed my arm and pulled me up.

"You're coming with me," Dr. Fric repeated, pulling me in front of him. With one arm, he held me close, and with his other he kept the ice pick at my temple.

Shit.

"Let go of me!" I yelled, not because I thought he would, but because I was hoping someone would hear me. And they did.

"Are you kidding me?" Spencer said, running to my rescue. He wasn't alone. Standing with an ice pick to my head had brought out the whole police force. I was happy to see that Arrow was with them and he was fine.

"Back off, or I'll stick this in her brain!" Dr. Fric growled.

"I've been there," Arrow said. "It's not good."

"I told you to sit tight. Why didn't you stay where I told you?" Spencer demanded, aiming his really big gun.

"I did!" I protested. "What are you doing with that gun?"

The doctor clutched me tighter. "I'll ram it in her brain! I swear it! Put your gun down!"

"He swears it and I believe him," I told Spencer. "Put your gun down!"

There was no clean shot. If anyone took a shot, I was either going to get hit, or I was going to get an ice pick in my head. There was no way out. Dr. Fric started to back up with me in front of him.

"Here's what's going to happen," he yelled so everyone could hear. "I'm taking her out of here in my car. Once I'm far enough away and I know that I'm not being followed, I'll release her. You hear me?"

"I hear you," Spencer said.

"Aren't you going to save me?" I asked.

"Nobody's going to save you," Dr. Fric sneered, as we walked backward toward the parking lot. "It's just me and you, and you better not do anything funny."

"I'm never funny," I said.

Spencer got further and further away as we walked slowly to the doctor's car. When we reached it, he unlocked it without lowering the ice pick. It looked like all was lost.

"What's that sound?" he asked.

"My blood pressure."

"No. Shh. The cops better not be pulling a fast one, or I swear I'll stick you like a shish kabob."

I didn't want to be a shish kabob, so I shut up and listened. It sounded like hail was hitting the blacktop. I looked up. There wasn't a cloud in the sky.

But the sound was getting louder. *Click. Click. Click. Click.* It sounded like a hailstorm, but there was no sign of hail.

"What's that over there?" Dr. Fric asked, his voice full of fear.

"What? Where?"

"Hurry. Get in the car. Hurry!"

Then, I saw what he was afraid of. The pack of wild chihuahuas was coming straight for us. The *click click* of their nails on the asphalt was getting louder. Now I heard the ding of the bells around a couple of their necks.

"They look angry," I said.

"Get in the car!"

I wasn't going to get in the car. I would rather take my chances with a pack of wild dogs than the ice pick.

I watched as the little dogs came at us with definite purpose. For some reason, I wasn't scared, and then I realized why. Each dog was focused entirely on Dr. Fric. They were coming for him, not me.

The doctor seemed to realize it too. He let me go and held the ice pick in a defensive posture against the chihuahuas. Behind the dogs, Spencer and his police came running. But they couldn't outrun the dogs.

When the pack of dogs reached us, they attacked Dr. Fric with a vengeance. He tried to stab them with the ice pick, but they bit his ankles and threw him off balance, making him drop his weapon. I jumped out of the melee to safety and watched as the doctor got a big shot of karma in the guise of tiny dogs of the rich and famous.

Dr. Fric screamed like a man being attacked by a pack of wild chihuahuas. Somehow, they managed to take him down, and once he was flat on his back in the parking lot, they jumped on him.

"It's a free for all," I called to Spencer, who had his mouth open. Waking out of a shocked stupor, he ordered his men to clear out the dogs and help the murderer-kidnapper.

Spencer walked to me, took me in his arms, and checked me for damage.

"The next time I tell you to stay put, don't listen to me, okay?" he said, gazing into my eyes.

I nodded. "Don't worry. I promise to never listen to you again."

"That's my girl," he said, and kissed me until every single chihuahua was rounded up and on its way to the Humane Society.

CHAPTER 15

*Ohm! Ohm! Hear that, bubeleh? Your Grandma is
meditating. Just kidding. I don't believe in sitting still.
You sit still too long at my age and folks start to think
you're dead. I'm not ready for that ending, although if it
did happen, it would be a happy ending. That's the problem
with happy endings...they're the end. But our matches want
that: a happy ending. Don't give it to them, dolly. Give them
a happy for now. A happy for now can last forever.*

*Lesson 112, Matchmaking advice from your
Grandma Zelda*

I woke up slowly. My bedroom was flooded with
sunlight, illuminating Spencer's naked body next to mine. He
was facing me, watching me, and as my eyes opened, he
pulled my leg over his waist.

"Good morning, beautiful," he greeted me.

I lifted my arm and stretched. "Is it still morning? I feel like I've been sleeping forever."

I had been sleeping on and off since we had left West Side Hospital. Spencer had been forced to work double-time, cleaning up the conspiracy and arresting people, but I had come home, taken a shower, and went to bed. Besides taking a few hours to eat takeout food that my grandmother had ordered in, I had spent most of my time in my room, under my covers.

"It's eleven-thirty," Spencer said. "Plenty of time to get ready for the wedding and to do other stuff."

He glided his fingers up my thigh to show me what he meant by "other stuff."

"I like other stuff," I said.

His hand moved to my lower back and pulled me in close. "Do you know what day it is?" he asked, his voice low and sexy as hell.

"It's Lucy's wedding day."

"And?"

"Sunday."

"And?"

"Other stuff day?"

Spencer smirked. "You're my kind of woman, Pinky. But no, it's Valentine's Day."

"Oh, no." I had totally forgotten about Valentine's Day. I hadn't bothered to get Spencer a card or a dirt bike or whatever girlfriends gave their boyfriends.

Spencer turned onto his back and stretched his arm out to pick up something from the floor. He handed me a bouquet of flowers, a large box of chocolate, and a small, rectangular jewelry box.

I stared at the box. "This is the first time in my life that I don't care about chocolate," I said.

"Open it."

I opened it. Inside was a brochure for an inn. I looked up at Spencer, questioningly.

"Our first vacation together. We're going next month," he explained.

"A vacation? A real one?"

"Are there other kinds?" he asked.

When I was a kid, my mother told me we were going on vacation, but we went to a casino, and I had to sit in the lobby and wait for her to seven out at craps, losing our rent money for the month. Other than that, I had never gone on a real vacation with a hotel and souvenirs.

"Can I get a souvenir while we're there?"

"A giant pencil? A magnet?"

"A snow globe!"

Spencer smirked. "A snow globe. Sure, Pinky."

"A vacation," I breathed. "I'm going on a vacation."

He touched the underside of my breast, caressing it with the back of his fingers. Then, he kissed me gently, sliding his tongue in my mouth. He pulled me underneath him, and I wrapped my legs around his waist. "We'll get away from this crazy town and sit back and do other stuff," he said, as he trailed light kisses over my face.

"I like other stuff," I said.

Before I got ready for the wedding, I helped my grandmother set up her "Valentine's Survivalist Day," which included two full meals, a Meg Ryan movie marathon, therapy sessions for those in dire need, and a series of beauty treatments.

I thought the beauty treatments were going to be

canceled because of Bird's nervous breakdown, and I was surprised to see her setting up in the sun room at the back of the house. She was looking much better. Her hair was done, and she was wearing makeup.

"Nice to see you, Bird," I said. "You're looking good."

She was ordering her staff around, setting up mani-pedi stations, a massage table, and a hairdressing chair. "Getting there, Gladie. I'm finally getting back to myself, and I'm hearing great things about a Hummus diet. When this is done, I'll get you the details on it."

"Thanks," I said and stepped out of the room, dreading trying the hummus diet.

I found my grandmother in the kitchen with about twenty matches, serving themselves from foil dishes filled with an assortment of potluck. "Want some macaroni and cheese, dolly?" she asked me. "It's delicious. But avoid the okra casserole," she whispered in my ear.

"I saw Bird," I said.

"She had an epiphany. Lucy's bald head did it. Bird couldn't let that happen to another woman in Cannes, again. She's now the Lone Ranger of hair care."

I nodded. It was too late for Lucy's hair, but the lonely townsfolk on Valentine's were going to get a lot of attention in order to make them feel better. All seemed right with the world.

I set up the television in the salon for the Meg Ryan marathon, and a couple of the matches laid out a layer of pillows on the floor for people to get comfortable while they watched the movies. After I turned the first movie on, I cleaned up lunch and took the trash out to the cans in front.

Outside, Bridget had arrived and was getting out of her car, carrying a dry cleaning bag. "I heard that Bird was doing hair, and I wanted a French braid," she explained.

I tossed the trash in the can. "Come inside. There's leftovers, too."

Bridget's stomach growled. "Thank goodness. Little Franklin makes me constantly hungry."

"Franklin? What happened to Vladimir?"

"Franklin Roosevelt created the Wagner Act, which was good for labor rights. Wagner's a good name, too. This is harder than you'd think, Gladie."

I put my arm around her shoulders and walked back to the house with her. "You have time. Maybe when you pop him out, he'll look more like a Wagner or more like a Franklin. Maybe you'll know then."

"You'd be a good godmother. Not that I believe in godmothers, but if I did, I would pick you to be my son's godmother. Gladie?"

"Yes?"

"Would you be Franklin's godmother?"

"I'd love to," I said, telling the truth. "Hey, guess where I'm going next month?"

"Hot mama in the house," Spencer whistled, when I left my bathroom. I was dressed in the hottest maid of honor dress that had ever been created. There was no space for a bra, and barely enough space for my breasts. The back dipped down to my butt, and the whole dress was one long peach-colored silk sheath.

"Do you think it's too much?" I asked him.

"Yes. Thank God."

"You don't look so bad, yourself," I said. He was wearing a beautifully-fitted tuxedo. He posed for me, and I almost stripped him down and made us late for Lucy's wedding.

"Harry hooked me up. This was Tony Two-fingers's suit, but he didn't get a chance to wear it. He was offed in the shower, and the tux was found laid out on the bed. Not a drop of blood on it. Can you believe it?"

Spencer drove Bridget and me to the wedding, which had been moved to Uncle Harry's property behind his McMansion up in the mountains outside of Cannes, where there was a security detail and no lake.

When we arrived, we found a parking crew, directing cars in front of the house. Spencer parked and helped Bridget and me out of the car. We were early, but there was still a stream of guests walking around the house to the back. I would have figured that with the rehearsal dinner catastrophe now an infamous part of town lore, that people would have avoided the wedding like the plague. But once again, curiosity got the best of people's good sense.

I was a little nervous, too. What else could go wrong?

"Warn me if you see a goat," I told Spencer.

"I heard that they nixed all animals for the ceremony and party," Bridget told me. "Ditto the portable heaters. Joannie Bush's cat can predict the weather, so they asked it about today, and the cat told them that it would be warm enough without the heaters. Why are you looking at me like that?"

Uncle Harry greeted us in the back. He was wearing a tuxedo and smoking a cigar. He was surrounded by goon bodyguards. "Congratulations," I told him.

"Thanks, Legs. Nice digs, right?"

The decorations were beautiful. Tables and chairs were laid out across the lawn. There was no tent to blow away. Each table had a large, intricate centerpiece, and there were flowers everywhere.

"We're keeping it simple this go around," Harry explained. "Would you mind going in to see Lucy? She's a bit nervous."

Bridget and I walked in, passing the wedding cake.

"Is that...?" I asked.

"I think it's a giant phallus," Bridget said. "Circumcised."

Uh oh. The baker struck again. This time, though, he had outdone himself. The cake was a towering achievement, completely erect with a confectionery spray of ejaculate that defied gravity.

I didn't think that Lucy would appreciate Mr. Frankenberry's new creation. So, I was expecting to see a completely drugged out, freaked out bride, but when we found her inside the house, Lucy surprised me.

"Did you see my dick cake?" she asked when we walked into her dressing room. She was wearing her wedding dress and headpiece, and she was giving Princess Grace a run for the money in the elegance department. "At least it's not a vagina cake, right?"

"Right," I said.

"And it's circumcised," Bridget said. "I'm debating the whole circumcision thing for little Franklin, though. Still, I bet your dick cake will be delicious."

"And you have a lot of security," I added. "That'll help the wedding to run smoothly."

Lucy checked herself out in the mirror. "Harry says that if anyone steps out of line, he'll shoot them. Quick and easy."

"That should work out well," I commented.

Just like Lucy said, the wedding ceremony was quick and easy. No drinks were served until Harry and Lucy were announced husband and wife. Cletus behaved and wasn't allowed to touch the wedding ring. The preacher didn't punch anyone out, and Harry didn't have to shoot anyone.

When the couple walked back down the aisle, Beyoncé appeared and sang an Aretha Franklin song, and Aretha Franklin appeared and sang a Bette Midler song. The crowd went wild, and there were a million iPhone pictures taken.

An hour later, Spencer and I were dancing on the dance floor. "I really like that dress. I can't wait for you to take it off," he said ogling me.

I was ready to take it off. I had had two glasses of champagne, that mixed with Spencer's wandering hands were making me ready to get naked with him.

"This is some party," I said. "I've never been to anything this fancy. But maybe we can sneak out early."

Bridget swayed to the music, making her way to us. "It's time for you to make your toast, Gladie," she said.

"My what?"

Bridget fanned herself. "Isn't the weather crazy? So hot. I heard that the snow up the mountain has completely melted."

"I have to make a toast?" I asked.

The music stopped, and the wedding planner clinked a spoon against a champagne glass to get the guests' attention.

Spencer walked with me to the band's stage where a microphone was waiting for me and my toast.

"You're going to be great," Spencer whispered in my ear. "The vortex has completely disappeared, and your tits are spectacular in that dress. Everyone's going to love you."

The wedding planner handed me the microphone. I felt faint, but I tried to keep it together. "Thank you all for coming," I said, my voice squeaking with nervousness. "Lucy has been a great friend. She's smart and put together, always traveling places for her marketing career…"

I gasped and shut my mouth. I had forgotten what "marketing" meant.

"I mean, the wedding is very nice, and there's no goats or lake, and Uncle Harry hasn't had to shoot anybody. There hasn't been one arrest, and nobody died. Sometimes that happens to me, you know. Finding dead people. Anyway…"

Help I mouthed to Spencer. I was going nowhere fast. I was going to ruin Lucy's wedding if I didn't shut up. My brain had melted, and it was drooling out of my mouth. Why was I given a microphone? I hadn't used a microphone since I was the tram tour guide at the Wildlife Park in Kansas City for two days. That didn't end well. Not with the tigers and all.

"Somebody save that girl, would you? It's like watching a rat chew its leg off to escape a trap," Ruth shouted from her seat.

Spencer put his arm around me and took the

microphone. "As Gladie said so eloquently, ladies and gentlemen, please raise your glasses and toast the beautiful couple. Lucy and Harry, may you enjoy a long lifetime of happiness. Cheers!"

Glasses were raised, and everyone took a sip. Lucy and Harry kissed, and Lucy had never looked happier.

Then, there was a scream. Then, another.

"It's the end of the world," one guest yelled.

Spencer looked down at me. "I'm not surprised. It's been nearly two hours without any mishaps. That's sort of a record, right?"

Bridget ran to me. "The snow melted, and it's flooding downhill. Look!"

She pointed at a series of eucalyptus trees, crashing to the ground, as a sea of water came toward us.

Spencer rolled his eyes. "A flood. Big deal."

"You're being awfully calm," I said. "No vortex comments. No 'are you kidding me.'"

Spencer seemed to think about that. "You're right. Maybe I've mellowed? Or maybe I'm drunk. How many drinks have I had?"

"Eight."

"Well, that's it, then. That's your answer."

"Get to higher ground," someone yelled, and Harry's friends began shooting at the rushing water. When their bullets ran out, they threw their guns at the water and ran for the hills. The guests scattered for higher ground, running around to the front of the house and up the street, where it was dry. Harry and Lucy invited us to go into his house and stick it out on the second-floor deck. About twenty other guests came with us.

"That fucking cat," Lucy growled, tapping her toe on the wooden deck.

"It did say a hot day, and it's hot," Bridget pointed out.

"The cat said it was a hot day, and it's hot," Spencer repeated to me, giving me his best smirk.

We looked down below, as a sea of water rushed below us. "It was a lovely wedding," I commented.

"I guess Gladie will be next," someone said, and I gasped and choked on my own spit.

"Easy there, girl," Ruth said. "Nobody's going to chain you up here and now."

"I know that, Ruth. I'm not scared about being…you know what." I couldn't even say the word, marriage.

"Yeah, right," she said.

"Anyway, next month Spencer is taking me on a vacation," I said, trying to change the subject. "A beautiful inn, and we're going to stop at the M&M's store on our way. I can't wait."

"M&M's store?" Ruth asked. "CVS is the M&M's store. Safeway is the M&M's store. This is America. Every store is the damned M&M's store. We should have a sign at the border: *Welcome to America. Help yourself to some M&M's.* This country is going down the toilet. M&M's store. M&M's store. A nation of morons, that's what we've become."

"Okay, Ruth. You veered off," I said.

"Well, you know what I mean."

"You sure are passionate about M&M's."

I took Spencer's hand, and we watched the water flow beneath the deck. The band had come inside and started to play a Beatles medley.

I smiled at Ruth, and she smiled back. I could always count on her to change the subject.

Don't miss **Scareplane**, *the next book in the Matchmaker Mysteries.*

SCAREPLANE

book seven of the matchmaker mysteries series

elise sax

And don't forget to sign up for the newsletter for new releases and special deals: http://www.elisesax.com/mailing-list.php

ABOUT THE AUTHOR

Elise Sax writes hilarious happy endings. She worked as a journalist, mostly in Paris, France for many years but always wanted to write fiction. Finally, she decided to go for her dream and write a novel. She was thrilled when *An Affair to Dismember*, the first in the *Matchmaker Mysteries* series, was sold at auction.

Elise is an overwhelmed single mother of two boys in Southern California. She's an avid traveler, a swing dancer, an occasional piano player, and an online shopping junkie.

Friend her on Facebook: facebook.com/ei.sax.9

Send her an email: elisesax@gmail.com

You can also visit her website: elisesax.com

And sign up for her newsletter to know about new releases and sales https://bit.ly/2PzAhRx

Made in the USA
Monee, IL
03 August 2023

40434444R00154